"POISON ME?" she gasped

CAMILLA LATHROP slumped into a chair. Her eyes widened in horror as Dr. Warren said: "Someone tried to kill you with one of the most deadly poisons known to man...."
The occasion was a tea party given by Dr. Hyssop, Master of Cambridge. Present were all those under suspicion of killing Julius Baumann, an honours student. But what frightened everyone was the fact that the girl's invitation to the party had been forged!
Baumann had died shortly after asking Hilary Fenton to mail an important letter for him. A second murder followed. Finally Camilla, Hilary's girl friend, came into the killer's orbit. From that moment, she lived a nightmare of terror—and no one knew when or where it would end....

Q. Patrick was one of the pseudonyms used by Richard Wilson Webb who wrote with a variety of writing partners either as Q Patrick, Quentin Patrick, or Jonathan Stagge. Murder at Cambridge, however, was written just by Richard Webb in 1932. Born in Somerset England Richard Wilson Webb spent the majority of his working life in the USA.

MURDER
at
CAMBRIDGE

Q. PATRICK

Ostara Publishing

First published in Great Britain 1932

Ostara Publishing edition 2012

A catalogue record for this book is available from the British Library

Every reasonable effort has been made by the Publisher to establish whether any person or institution holds the copyright for this work. The Publisher invites any persons or institutions that believe themselves to be in possession of any such copyright to contact them at the address below.

Some of the words used and views expressed in this text, in common usage when originally published, could be considered offensive today. The Publishers have reproduced the text as published but would wish to emphasise that such words and terms in no way represent the views and opinions of the Publisher.

ISBN 9781906288747

Printed and Bound in the United Kingdom

Ostara Publishing
13 King Coel Road
Colchester
CO3 9AG
www.ostarapublishing.co.uk

GLOSSARY

For the benefit of those who have not sojourned long at Cambridge, some of the local colloquialisms and other quasi-technical terms used in this book are explained below.

Absit (Latin—"let him be absent"): Permission to stay away from Cambridge for one day. Absence must not be extended after midnight.

Aegrotat (Latin—"he is sick"): Permission to suspend university activities or postpone examinations because of illness.

Bedmaker: A college servant (female). Almost always abbreviated to "bedder."

Blood: A colloquialism for an expert at athletics—an athletic snob. The term usually implies a somewhat over-careful selection of clothes and intimates.

Blue: Light blue at Cambridge and dark blue at Oxford are the colours given to those undergraduates who have represented their university in one of the major sports (boat-racing, cricket, football, etc.) in an inter-'Varsity contest. A blue has been described as "a hall-mark of intellectual inefficiency." It is nothing of the sort.

Bull Dog: A college servant, usually youngish and fleet of foot who accompanies the proctor on his prowlings. They go in couples, wear tophats and are scrupulously polite. But they get there just the same.

Combination Room: A mysterious chamber in which the fellows of the college assemble to drink port after Hall. No one has ever yet discovered what they talk about there, but the conversation is reputed to be very brilliant. It has been described alternately as "the unwritten history of England" and "the unprintable history of Cambridge."

C. U. A. D. S.: Cambridge University Amateur Dramatic Society.

Debag: Forcibly to remove the trousers (someone else's). Usually accompanied by other playful badinage.

Don: A generic term for fellows, tutors and heads of colleges. The freshman is apt to confuse these gentlemen with the "gyps." A simple rule to remember is: "The gyp is the tidier individual." (Freshman's Guide.)

Exeat (Latin—"let him go away"): Permission to leave Cambridge over night.

Girton: See Newnham.

Gyp: A college servant (male) usually assigned to take care of a certain set of rooms or the rooms of one particular staircase. Strangely enough, the name bears absolutely no relationship to the American slang word which is spelt the same. (At Oxford it is pronounced *scout.*)

Hall: The college dining hall. A large building usually remarkable for its architecture and portraits of illustrious alumni. Dining in Hall is more or less compulsory, hence "after Hall," merely means after the evening meal.

High Table: A raised table in Hall reserved for dons, fellows and their guests. The food served is no better there—but the drinks are!

K. C: King's Counselor.

K. P.: King's Parade. A main street in Cambridge.

Littlego: The entrance examination which must be passed by all before being admitted to Cambridge University. There is no royal road for athletes. (Oh, yeah!)

Marlborough: A famous English public school.

Mays: End of year examinations usually held in May. There is nothing final about them but they are often fatal.

M. C. C: Marylebone Cricket Club. A famous London cricket eleven always referred to by its initials, possibly because the correct pronunciation of the word is too difficult for ordinary use.

Newnham (and **Girton):** The two women's colleges at Cambridge. Officially females have no rights in the government of the University except inasmuch as they often marry the fellows, graduates and undergraduates, thus getting around it in another way. The percentages of such marriages is probably higher at Cambridge than at Oxford, since in the University, the girls are obliged to wear very unbecoming caps and gowns!

Oak: The usual set of college rooms at Cambridge has two doors. The outer one—or oak—is very thick, and when "sported" (closed), this is the polite English way of saying, "Keep out—this means YOU."

Proctor: A don dressed up as a policeman. He prowls about, usually-after dark, accompanied by two bulldogs (see above) and maintains discipline by fining luckless or gownless undergraduates six shillings and eightpence or multiples thereof. Verb, (tr.) *Prog.*

R. A. M. C.: Royal Army Medical Corps.

Special: (1) The shortest and easiest cut to a B. A. Degree. (2) The shortest and easiest cut to intoxication via Beer.

Sport: See Oak (above).

Tripos (Derivation from Greek words meaning "three feet"): A university examination for the B. A. Degree. Usually—and very suitably—abbreviated to Trip.

Union: The famous debating hall at Cambridge. The "home of lost causes" and the cause of several (to my knowledge) lost homes!

'Varsity: Simply an abbreviation of the word University. It has no athletic or other sinister significance.

CHAPTER I

"I Am Born"

In the flat but not altogether unpleasing Fen country, about sixty miles northeast of London, lies the small market town of Cambridge. If you have an Oxford tradition in the family, you may have heard that it achieved a certain amount of notoriety as a seat of learning during the Middle Ages.

Should you chance to possess an uncle or a cousin who was a Rhodes scholar, he may have casually mentioned the fact that Cambridge University is now devoted almost entirely to the winning of boat races and the mass production of marvelous, if somewhat moronic, athletes.

If, as a tourist, you are a disciple of the ubiquitous Baedeker, you will probably know even less than this. For, in his discussion of the University towns of England, after a glowing and lengthy tribute to the beauties of Oxford, he summarily dismisses her less ostentatious sister with the curt phrase—"If pressed for time, Cambridge may be omitted."

After which modest preamble on the subject of my Alma Step-Mater, I feel that I am now perfectly justified in diverting my reader's attention entirely towards myself.

My name is Fenton, but you had better call me Hilary. Somehow or other I don't seem to smell as sweet by the name which my godfathers and godmothers saw fit to bestow on me at my baptism, viz., Hilarion Aloysius. I am at present an undergraduate in residence at All Saints College. Cantab., where I am ostensibly studying English.

My real purpose, however, is to polish off any odd corners that may have survived four years at Harvard. I am, amongst other things, a native of Philadelphia and consequently an American citizen.

But when I imply that I was born in Philadelphia, I am using the word in its most crass, material and corporeal sense. Mentally, spiritually and emotionally, I was born in a Cambridge lecture room at about 10:15AM on a certain Monday halfway through the May term. My birth, I might add, took place in the twenty-fourth year of my life.

That was the exact moment when all the trouble really started, and if any enterprising pathologist should happen, in the (I hope) fairly distant future, to perform an autopsy on my remains, he will find this particular date scrawled across my heart in letters of flame and magenta.

The fateful day dawned clear and surprisingly warm for May. No comets, no fall of meteorites had occurred during the night to announce the portentous happenings with which it was to be so richly fraught. I rose reasonably early. On returning from the half mile or so which usually separates the inmate of a Cambridge college from his bath, I caught a glimpse of the Cam, still winding peacefully along between its daisied banks.

I could hear the majestic notes of a Bach chorale from the organ in Kings Chapel. An occasional undergraduate sauntered across the old gray pavements of the court—the bright colours of his bathrobe forming a striking contrast against the encrusted stones of the college building.

Black-coated servants carried heavily laden breakfast trays up oaken staircases and a cluster of white surplices announced that chapel was over. In short, everything was just as usual, and the University was turning over in bed and opening one sleepy eye exactly as it had in the days of Queen Elizabeth.

"A" staircase, however, had not yet done more than merely stretch itself, and the only people stirring were Hank, our solemn gyp, and Mrs. Bigger, who performed the mystic offices of bedmaker. These I saluted with democratic cordiality and then proceeded to my room where I ate an uneventful egg over an antiquated copy of *The New Yorker*.

All this was punctuated at rare intervals by glimpses into Blake's *Songs of Innocence*, in leisurely anticipation of a lecture I was to attend that morning. At about 9:30 I tucked under my arm the abbreviated gown required by the authorities for all those *in statu pupillari* and strolled downstairs.

That all this sounds terribly trite and trivial, I am well aware. And yet, in the light of future events, every triviality which occurred that morning, in fact, almost everything which occurred that day, later became gravid with significance and rich with sinister possibility.

As I reached the ground floor, I almost collided with a tall, fair-haired youth in gorgeous sky-blue pyjamas. An arm, languid yet muscular, was thrown around my neck and I felt myself forcibly propelled into a room redolent of roasting coffee, Virginia cigarettes and Yardley's shaving soap. A *Daily Mail* was thrust into my hand as a harsh, nasal voice, supposedly in imitation of my transatlantic accent, said mockingly:

"Take a peek at that, kid. It sure will send your old man."

I glanced at the paragraph indicated and then up into the smiling blue eyes of my persecutor. Stuart Somerville was one of those blond young giants who are sent to Cambridge with the express purpose of giving inferiority complexes to us scrubby individuals of five feet nine or thereabouts.

Always perfectly dressed, perfectly poised and perfectly sure of themselves, they exhale the very essence of the English remnants of the feudal system. They are the fruit of cricket and cold tubs. In later life they talk about Empire, write letters to *The Times,* and invariably they think about—nothing. They are decorative but dumb; lovely but limited.

Stuart Somerville, however, had broadened his horizon somewhat by an athletic trip to America and enjoyed nothing better than practicing the vernacular on me. His memory with regard to Bowery slang was remarkable and, where memory failed, the movies and detective stories had stepped in to fill the breach.

"I really see nothing in the paper that would be of special interest to my father," I said, with what dignity I could muster under the circumstances. "And I wish—"

Stuart ran a hand through his dishevelled, corn-colored hair and raised his eyebrows in mock-surprise.

"So Hilary doesn't read pappy's law books, eh? Well, get a load of this, buddy. William North has escaped. He's done one beautiful big bunko. And all after your inestimable pop had made him figure so large in the dullest of all his dull text-books, Fenton's *Famous Second Trials.*"

I was used to this kind of nonsense from Stuart and it was, to some extent, justifiable. He was reading for a "special" in Law and thus was constantly victimized by Fenton on Torts, Fenton's *Legal Theory* and the aforementioned *Famous Second Trials.* That my father, though a perfectly good American, was a sometime fellow of All Saints and a well-known writer of law books was considered by most people to be my misfortune rather than my fault.

They kindly overlooked this blot on my family escutcheon. But Stuart Somerville never let me forget it. The sins of my father were repeatedly visited on me, even though they had been committed a full generation ago—before marriage with my mother had put mayonnaise on the paternal salad days once and for all.

My father now sat lofty and unassailable on the bench of the United States Supreme Court. His lectureship at Cambridge had long ago ended, but his text-books lingered on to be thorns in the flesh of the budding barrister and the embryo K.C.

And so, whenever Stuart Somerville saw any reference to my father or to one of the cases which he had used as illustrations in his text-books, he took an unholy delight in drawing my attention to the matter. This reverberation from the once famous North trial was a typical case in point.

"I wish," I said at length, "you would let my poor father alone for awhile. It's not his fault that North has got out and it's certainly not my fault that the Cambridge Law School is still antiquated enough to use his text-books. Supposing I were to make scathing remarks about your father every time I see a cow or a turnip." (Sir Anthony Somerville owns about one half of Cambridgeshire.)

Stuart gave a whoop of delight at this feeble sally and promptly threw me down on the couch and sat on me for several very uncomfortable minutes. As he did so, he improved the shining hour with some pregnant remarks about the moulting of the American eagle and the prowess of the British lion.

I finally escaped from his room and proceeded to my lecture in a thoroughly dishevelled condition. Even in my most intellectual moments I am not capable of appreciating the somewhat exotic mysticism of William Blake; and I was certainly in no mood for it that morning.

I managed, however, to listen attentively for the first few minutes while the lecturer explained that the famous poem about the Sunflower was in no sense of the word botanical, but that it really symbolized a sex repression or the early symptoms of pernicious anemia. After that my thoughts began to wander and I found myself looking along the row of faces.

There were thoughtful youths in old tweeds; boys with fresh complexions, boys with spotty faces—the usual assortment. Then there was the sprinkling of girls from Newnham and Girton, most of them wearing particularly unsightly hats.

All, so it seemed, had pencils working overtime on any tit-bits of solid fact that might advantageously be reproduced in an examination paper. I saw nothing new or exciting. I was rather bored. My brain was lethargic. My hands were idle and Satan was undoubtedly cooking up some mischief.

And then, all of a sudden, out of a sea of ordinary, everyday faces, I caught a glimpse of the Profile. Up to now it had been concealed behind the rather prominent girl in spectacles. At first I thought it must be just a phantasy bred of some obscure wish-fulfilment complex.

I didn't, I couldn't believe that it really existed in a musty old Cambridge lecture room. And yet, there it was standing out from the rest like a scarlet tanager among a flock of sparrows. Nothing that I had seen before had ever seemed so perfect.

Probably she didn't measure up to the world's most rigid standards of perfection. But which of the famous heroines of history really did? There is documentary evidence to prove that Cleopatra was positively plain; that Mélisande was an untidy creature with wispy hair and staring eyes, and that Juliet was a long-legged and precocious sub-deb of about fourteen.

And yet each of these ladies appeared as visions of light and beauty to Anthony, Pelléas and Romeo respectively. They set a fashion for love at first sight and now who shall dare to say that such cannot exist? Perhaps it is only at first sight (as the cynics have told us) that perfect beauty can exist.

To me the Profile seemed perfectly and utterly beautiful. The contours were classical without being severe. The nose, coming down in an almost straight line from the forehead, was Greek rather than Roman. The line of the cheek was clearly yet delicately marked. A curve of dark hair was just visible beneath a plain and perfectly negligible hat. The complexion was clear olive.

I could not see the colour of her eyes. But, as I twisted my head in a vain effort to find out, something absurd seemed to be happening inside of me. In that one hyperbolic moment I felt that I was really seeing things for the first time in my life.

I seemed to understand, in a flash, what the poets had been writing about all down the centuries. Even the obscurity of William Blake became amazingly clear. I knew what pictures were about. The whole of art, music and life stood suddenly revealed.

I was in love. But surely it was not really I who was experiencing these tempestuous feelings. Not the Hilary Fenton whose only emotional experiences to date were to hear the Philadelphia

Orchestra and to hand out a rapid line to hard-boiled Radcliffe girls. It was—it must be—a new Hilary Fenton. Someone utterly different. Some strange, primitive creature who had suddenly become overpoweringly and sensuously alive on a warm, steel-blue day in spring—at Cambridge—in a lecture room with thirty or forty other undergraduates; alive and alone with the Profile.

A piece of paper was thrust towards me by my neighbour. It was the attendance list. Immediately my mind snapped back into action and I did some of the fastest mental arithmetic since my prep school days. I counted the names backwards. Jean Higginbotham—that was the girl who came first. Camilla Lathrop—that must be the prominent one with the spectacles. Dorothy Dupuis—that must be the name which a stupid world applied to the Profile. I pushed the paper away from me.

"Aren't you going to sign it?" whispered the solemn young man by my side.

I had forgotten to add my own name to the list. Just as I scribbled Hilary Fenton across the page with a brand new, triumphant kind of flourish, I caught the prophetic voice of the lecturer rising loud and clear above the tumult of my emotions.

"O Rose, thou art sick!
The invisible worm
That flies in the night,
In the howling storm,

"Has found out thy bed
Of crimson joy;
And his dark secret love
Does thy life destroy."

The lecture was over. I made a rush towards the door but a milling group of chattering undergraduates temporarily barred my passage. I pushed and shoved, and when I finally reached the court, I was only just in time to catch a glimpse of the Profile in the distance, as she slipped on a quite unnecessary raincoat and hurried across Clare Bridge with the prominent girl in spectacles.

Pursuit would have been both useless and undignified. She had gone as suddenly as she came, but I didn't seem to care. I knew her name. I knew she must be reading English and I knew the way her chin joined on to her throat. That was quite enough to go on with.

There were no more lectures on my schedule for that morning, so I strolled back towards my own college, puffing at a meditative pipe. As the hazy smoke ascended in the clear May sunshine, vista upon vista seemed to be opening up in my imagination—and at the end of each one was inscribed the magic name, Dorothy Dupuis.

Skilfully avoiding the bicycles in Trinity Street, I kept repeating it over and over again. It didn't seem to suit the Profile in the very least. Somehow or other, I vaguely connected the name with an incident that didn't suit her either. For a few moments the half memory of that incident tortured me, hanging on the brink of my conscious mind. Then it began to come back to me.

It was at the dinner party given by the American Ambassador last vacation. What was her name—the stout lady who sat next to me at table and snorted over her soup? Lady—Lady Lusinger, that was it! I could hear her distinctly now:

"So you are up at Cambridge, young man. Well, I have a niece there too. The men in our family go to Oxford, of course. (Snort.) But Dorothy Dupuis is a very sensible sort of girl. I might say a thoughtful girl. (Two snorts.)"

The adjective might perhaps have been more suitably applied to the mackintosh rather than to the girl and I remembered how they had made me wince at the time. In fact, I had made an inward resolve that Dorothy Dupuis' acquaintance would not add to the gaiety of nations. But now I blessed the American Ambassador and his dull dinner party. I blessed Lady Lusinger and I blessed every snort that she had snorted. I felt absurdly happy.

And being happy, I had the natural instinct to share my happiness with someone else. But there was only one person at Cambridge to whom I ever talked about myself and that was Michael Grayling, who occupied the room directly below mine on "A" stair-case. He was my best and most intimate friend at college, but for the last few weeks he had been almost as difficult of approach as my next door neighbour, Julius Baumann, who lived on the fourth floor.

The two of them were working in deadly rivalry for the Lenox Open Scholarship—Michael because he really needed the money to complete his third year at Cambridge—Baumann because he wanted to fling his success in the world's teeth and prove that he was not only a marvelous cricketer but a considerable classical scholar as well.

It was with some surprise, therefore, that I saw Michael's door standing invitingly open as I passed up the stairs. He looked up from Plato's *Republic* as I entered the room. His brown eyes, I noticed, seemed very tired and there were faint parallel lines on his broad, bulgy forehead. My friend's smile of welcome, however, was as warm and sunny as ever.

"Doing a spot of work for a change," he announced in the apologetic tone assumed by even the most serious minded undergraduate when caught red-handed at his studies. "I'm past all help from lectures now and have to plug along by myself in the hopes that I'll hit on something that they will set in the papers. Not that I have an earthly chance, anyhow—unless Baumann dies or gets laid out in the Varsity Match against the M. C. C. this week."

The tone was light, but I knew the deep seriousness of his situation. The race, in this case, was to the swift. Baumann was brilliant; Michael was only a very creditable plodder. I made sympathetic noises with the roof of my mouth and was just about to divert my friend from his Plato with a description of the lecture and its quite unplatonic consequences, when a noise on the stairway above made me turn to look out of the door.

Now a noise on the stairway could mean only one thing—a visitor for me. Baumann, the misanthropic man of mystery, never had visitors. A constantly sported oak and a sullen scowl barred my South African neighbour from all friendly intercourse with his fellow men.

With a muttered excuse, I went out on to the third floor landing and left Michael to his Platonic ideals. Light footsteps were coming down from the fourth floor; a turn in the staircase revealed the fact that our visitor was a woman. Nor was it, as might have been expected, the inestimable Mrs. Bigger.

No, it was a young woman—a girl—a girl in a shabby rain coat, and, yes—heavens, how my heart was beating—it was the Profile. The Profile on our staircase, on my floor!

But now she was the Profile no longer, for this time I caught her head on, as it were. In the twinkling of a second I took in the interesting facts that her eyes were dark blue and that her full face did more than justice to the promise of the side view. I also noticed that a worried, unhappy expression had supplanted the earlier serenity of the lecture room.

She was holding a handkerchief in her hand and somehow I had the impression that she had just been using it to remove the trace of tears. (I was in far too romantic a frame of mind even to imagine that she might have a cold in the nose!) Or perhaps she kept it there to conceal a perfectly natural embarrassment for, despite musical comedies and the co-educational movies, women students are *not* in the habit of running around in the men's colleges at Cambridge.

As she came toward me, I thought of a thousand marvelous things to do. I thought of a thousand marvelous things to say. It was an heroic moment, but like most of life's great opportunities it was destined to be wasted. The mountains of my emotion had been in labor—a ridiculous mouse of conversation was born.

"Were you looking for someone?" was my final fatuity.

For a moment her eyes darkened with a look of annoyance and suspicion. The finely-marked eyebrows seemed almost to meet in the centre of her forehead and then her whole face suddenly smoothed itself out into a delightful smile.

"No—yes," she hesitated. "I wanted to—er—see Professor Long. He's on this staircase, isn't he?" Normally her voice must have been charming. It now sounded strained and a trifle husky.

"Professor Long is on the ground floor," I replied, "but he's only in his rooms on Saturday mornings." Everyone in Cambridge knew that Dr. Long, being almost ninety, kept very restricted office hours.

"Thanks." The handkerchief had now been put away and her smile was positively mischievous. "And—and lectures on Blake are well worth listening to, by the way. They are not intended as opportunities to stare at one's neighbours."

"Oh, I say, I'm sorry. But—but—" here I wanted to tell her about the line of her nose and forehead, the curve of her cheek and the full, devastating effect of her profile. They seemed sufficient reason for staring at anyone. Involuntarily, however, I chose a more conventional line, and stammered out, "—But you see, I know you. That is, I know your name. I know Lady Lusinger, and she told me—"

"And can I flatter myself that you deliberately followed me up here?" The tone was light but I thought I detected a note of anxiety beneath its lightness.

"Oh, no—I mean, yes. Well, I don't know what I mean, but my name is Hilary Fenton and that's my room up there behind you and, well, couldn't we have a date for lunch?"

"A date for lunch!" She laughed. "It sounds like a vegetarian food crank. I loathe dates. Why not a prune and have done with it? But—" here she paused and looked straight at me for the first time, "—you must be an American."

"I admit the allegation and admire the—er—perspicacity of the alligator," I said facetiously. She gave me a rather wintry smile and proceeded to edge past me down the stairs. My voice rose imploringly:

"Seriously though, I really am not a rounder—I mean bounder. I *do* know you—or, at least, your name. You're Dorothy Dupuis. I saw it on the attendance list. And Lady Lusinger did tell me to look you up."

She paused and her smile was so bright that I had the uncomfortable feeling that she was laughing at me rather than with me.

"Well, I must dash on now or I'll be late for a lecture in Kings— on the Pre-Raphaelites. I couldn't possibly have lunch with you today, but if you're really sure you know me, ask me some other time. Drop me a line at Clough Hall, Newnham."

Once again the handkerchief was produced and held up to her divine little Doric nose. She gave it a substantial blow and then passed on quickly down the stairs.

She was gone: but the fragrance of her stayed with me. It was a surprising and unforgettable fragrance, different from anything that I had ever smelled before. It was not English. It was not French. Nor was it Oriental. Exciting without being extravagantly exotic, it hung about the age-old staircase like a faint memory of half-gotten flowers or a romance of long ago.

But I did not stay to appreciate it. I was seized with a mad desire to catch a last glimpse of her. I wanted just to see her cross the court and go out by the gate. Accordingly I put my head out of the landing window which gave a good view of the only exit to our staircase. I waited five, I waited ten minutes. Still she did not appear.

At the end of half an hour she came out and walked quickly across the court. I noticed that she still held her handkerchief in one hand. She had missed her lecture on the Pre-Raphaelites. She was walking away from Kings. Dr. Long had not been in his room that morning and yet she had been half an hour on our staircase since leaving me. What had she been doing? When I pulled in my head and started upstairs again, her perfume was still with me. I have always been very sensitive to perfumes. I was destined never to forget this one.

CHAPTER II

Beg O' My Neighbour

Of all the many dignitaries and functionaries that play a part in the life of a Cambridge undergraduate, perhaps the least appreciated is his bedmaker. Cruel things have been sung and written about "bedders." Their very name lends itself to ridicule and unkind jokes. They are mocked for the better days which they invariably claim to have seen.

They are castigated for their taking ways—no heel tap, no remnant of tea, butter or sugar is supposed to be safe from their pilfering fingers. I have even heard them accused of being superannuated Girtonians who once took the wrong turning in youth and are now expiating their peccadillos by lives of service and sacrifice. They are, indeed, a much maligned race.

But the sublime Mrs. Bigger of "A" staircase cared for none of these things. She was, in every sense of the word, a bigger and better bedder, and I freely admit that she contributed not a little to my amusement and comfort while I was at Cambridge. In fact, until my encounter with the Profile, she was the nearest approach to a soft, feminine influence in this rugged phase of my life.

Perhaps some womanly intuition had warned Mrs. Bigger that there was a rival near her throne on that Monday morning. Perhaps she took exception to the unconventional hours which the Profile chose to wander about the staircase—at any rate, when I returned to my room, I found the good lady showing unmistakable symptoms of the tantrums which she usually reserved for Hank, her boss, or the unneighbourly Baumann, who was notoriously the thorn in her ample flesh.

"Hembarrassed," she sniffed, as she emerged from my bedroom with much indignant rustling of grey alpaca, "hembarrassed, that's wot I was, Mr. Fenton! To be caught a-empt'ing the slops by a young lady in the middle of the morning. I could of blushed for the shame of it."

(Mrs. Bigger's sentiments mirror to some extent the views of a great University that does not officially recognize the existence of women students.)

"Do you mean that she came into my room, Mrs. Bigger?" I asked, trying hard to conceal the eagerness of my curiosity.

The purple ostrich plume on her hat quivered with indignation and outraged decorum.

"No, hindeed, sir," replied the good lady in the tone which was first used on Eve by the Angel with the Flaming Sword. "Nobody comes into your room when you ain't here, Mr. Fenton—honly hover my dead body, sir. Leastways unless it's one of yer pertickler friends like Mr. Grayling or Mr. Comstock—folks as has a right on this staircase, sir."

"The young lady wasn't looking for me, then," I asked innocently.

Mrs. Bigger sniffed volubly. "I don't know wot she was 'ere for, Mr. Fenton, and that's a fact. A few minutes 'fore you come in, I went out and saw 'er on the stairs. But seein' as how I 'ad the pail in me 'and, I popped back into yer bedroom and waited as was only modest."

I casually remarked that our visitor had at least been remarkably easy on the eyes.

"'Andsome is as 'andsome does," replied my bedmaker cryptically, "and certainly she's 'andsome enough for that there Mr. Baumann. Not that she's as pretty as Mary Smith—'er as works as 'ousemaid over to the Master's Lodge—the girl as Mr. 'Ankin 'as honored with 'is attentions—"

She sniffed again, then added generously, "Haristocratic is the word I would of used for the young lady on the stairs, Mr. Fenton. Haristocratic she was almost to the point of bein' 'orty! As soon as I kleps me eyes on 'er, I says to meself, 'Well, mebbe she ain't dressed like a lady, but you'd never mistake 'er for one.'"

She paused on her way to the door. "But—I don't 'old with them mecks on a young woman! I onst 'ad a niece as wore a meck, Mr. Fenton, and she come to no good, she didn't. Two buckles," she added darkly. (Mrs. Bigger had a decided weakness for pathological conditions and their nomenclature and was never so happy as when she was describing the complicated diseases which carried off her friends and relatives.)

Having fired her Parthian shot at the objectional mackintosh, my bedmaker stalked from the room with one hand on her hip and the other clasping the handle of the aforementioned pail. Her departing gait, therefore, combined the lilt of Patience with the dignity of a prominent royal personage who is also to be seen wearing ostrich plumes in her hat.

After she had left me I felt that I could not settle down to work until I had written to the Profile. And while I am on the subject of work, I want to set at rest, once and for all, the anxiety which my over-conscientious readers will doubtless feel with regard to my studies during the course of this narrative.

I am naturally of a fairly studious turn of mind. But I had not come to Cambridge to shun delights and live laborious days exclusively. In fact my tutor had said to me some time previously, "You won't get a first, Fenton, not if you stand on your head until the date of the Tripos. You can't fail to get a second even if you stand on your head throughout the whole examination. Read the things you enjoy and develop your own taste.

"But don't overdo it or get a one-track mind. Just browse in the pastures that suit you best, but vary your diet and always get your full quota of vitamins such as Shakespeare, Milton, Donne and Wordsworth ..." In short, I was predestined to mediocrity. My leisurely attitude had the divine sanction of authority. I had no reason to be worried or hag-ridden.

I was worried now, however, as to my best method of approach in writing to the Profile. I had had so little experience with English girls and all my preconceived notions with regard to the British had been proved hopelessly wrong to date. It is not surprising, therefore, that I tore up several highly coloured flights of fancy and wasted nearly half a ream of crested note paper before I finally evolved the following piece of plain, straightforward prose:

Dear Miss Dupuis,

At a dinner party given by the American Ambassador last vacation I had the pleasure of meeting your aunt, Lady Lusinger. She told me that you were at Newnham and suggested that we might meet. I shall be at the "Whim" to-morrow (Tuesday) at one o'clock and shall be delighted if you can join me for lunch.

Sincerely,

Hilary Fenton.

There was nothing in this sober missive at which even Lady Lusinger herself could do more than give one of her milder variety of snorts. It was a harmless elixir of milk and water. I addressed it to Clough Hall, Newnham, and ran down to catch the twelve o'clock post.

It was when I returned to my room, some minutes later, that there occurred the second amazing incident of that already amazing day. As I pushed open my door I found to my intense surprise that Julius Baumann, my misanthropic neighbour, was standing by my fireplace obviously waiting for my return.

Now, to those whose jaded appetites require the constant stimulus of thrills and horror, I am afraid that this chronicle to date must have appeared hopelessly dull and singularly devoid of dramatic incident. A very ordinary (if American) undergraduate has attended a lecture where he has "fallen for" a girl to whom he has subsequently spoken.

He has written her a politely conventional letter, posted it and returned to find another undergraduate waiting in his room. Nothing in that to make a song about—let alone a mystery story. No? Well, the unexpected happens so seldom at Cambridge.

Today it had happened twice, and yet these extraordinary happenings afterwards seemed like the quiet lull before the storm of strange incidents that were to follow—mere *hors d'oeuvres* preceding a regular orgy of unexpectedness.

It should also be borne in mind that I had lived within twenty yards of Baumann for two and a half terms and he had never once passed my portal nor invited me to pass his. No shortage of cigarettes, no desire for a convivial sundowner, no primal urge for human companionship had led the South African to accord me more than a non-committal grunt when chance brought us face to face upon the staircase.

Nor, indeed, had I ever known him to be more civil to others. His only friend was Hank, the gyp, whose claim to notice lay in the fact that he, too, came from the Orange Free State and could converse with Baumann in a strange language called Afrikaans. Nothing could have surprised me more than to find this arch recluse leaning against my mantelpiece and staring at me from dark, sombre eyes.

"Fenton," he said abruptly in this thick, guttural accent. "I want to speak to you. Can you come into my room for a moment?"

I was so astonished that I could do nothing but open my mouth and shut it again. I seemed incapable of making any intelligible reply. However, there must have been a certain amount of antagonism in my speechlessness, for he seemed to think it necessary to urge me a second time.

"Please," he said, and there was a note almost of anguish in his voice. He was no longer the brilliant athlete whose cricket everyone admired and envied, no longer the fine classical scholar who was going to win the Lenox Scholarship and sail into an easy "first" in the Tripos—he was just a human being in what appeared to be a bad jam and, somehow or other, I could not gainsay him.

"Okay," I said quietly and followed him into his unfamiliar room. He shut the door behind us and sported his oak. As I sat down and lighted a cigarette to regain my composure, he stared at me so hard and so intensely that a feeling of annoyance and embarrassment crept over me.

"When you get your eyes full, fill your pockets," I remarked flippantly, the phrase occurring to me out of some dim, kindergarten memory.

He ignored my infantile banality.

"Fenton," he said, starting to pace up and down the floor, "before I ask you to do what I called you in here for, I want you to swear that you will never, under any circumstances, tell anyone in the world ..."

"Stop being so dramatic," I interrupted impatiently. "Of course I won't tell."

"But you swear?"

"Not often, but I will—if you insist."

"All right. I trust you. I suppose I have to. First of all I want you to witness my signature on a document here."

I nodded. He opened the door and called out to Hankin who came up from the landing below. Then the South African signed his name and the gyp and I solemnly affixed our own signatures. The proceeding was simple enough and certainly not sufficient to justify all the fuss and tumult.

When we were left alone together, Baumann folded up the document and remarked solemnly, "And now I want to tell you that I am probably going to have to leave Cambridge."

"*Exeat, absit* or *aegrotat?*" I asked, mentioning the only three methods by which one can leave Cambridge without spoiling one's chance of a degree. I was rather proud of being able to use a sentence composed almost entirely of Latin words to a classical scholar.

"If I go at all, I'm going down for good," he replied curtly.

Now this was news—real front page stuff, if you like. News of importance in the very highest circles, athletic and academic.

Baumann was by far the most consequential undergraduate at All Saints.

"But what about the Varsity match against the M. C. C. this week?" I stammered.

"So much the better for that cocky ass, Somerville. I don't suppose he will object very strongly to taking my place on the team." The corners of his mouth drooped in an acid smile.

"But the Lenox scholarship?" I asked again, and this time I could not conceal my interest in his reply. "You must be crazy to give up your chances of that, Baumann."

"Make things a bit easier for your pal, Grayling," he remarked. "That's about all I have to offer you in return for what I am going to ask you to do for me. It's not that I am considering either Somerville or Grayling themselves—you can be sure of that. They're like the rest of these blasted Englishmen.

"They hate me because I happen to be good at the things on which they fancy they have a monopoly; they despise me because I don't interest myself in what they call their college activities— because I don't waste my time drinking tea with a lot of stupid undergraduates...."

This was too much for me. I am no blind or besotted Anglophile—nor do I subscribe to the popular fallacy that the Battle of Waterloo was won on the playing fields of Eton—but I still feel that there is something to be said for England and her educational institutions.

"I think," I said coolly, as I threw my cigarette into the fireplace and rose from my chair, "that you had better ask favours from some *stupid undergraduate* of your own nationality. I am an American but I do happen to be at an English University. Both you and I have come over here to do or be done by Cambridge, Baumann. It has been remarkably generous to you. And as for me, I happen to like it. My best friends are English. Cheerio!" My hand was on the door knob.

"Machtig!" he muttered between his teeth, as he jumped up to stop me. "I'm sorry, Fenton, but I let my feelings get the better of me for a moment. You see, I'm a Dutchman—a Boer. The English have always treated us badly. We don't love them, we ..."

"We might try staying in our own country then," I remarked, but I could not help feeling sorry for this creature who was so warped and twisted with bitterness—for a man so friendless that he was obliged to ask favours of a total stranger. Besides, there had been a note of genuine homesickness in his voice.

I sat down again.

"I am going back," he cried, in a tone that was at once exultant and resentful. "I hate to leave just before I've got what I came for, but I see no other way out. Don't ask me my reasons."

"'He who has drunk of Afric's fountains will surely drink again,'" I quoted lightly. "And—incidentally—I'm in a heck of a hurry. I'm due to lunch with Comstock in ten minutes."

"Don't worry, I won't keep you long."

He went over to his desk and started to slip some papers into an envelope. I caught a crackling sound suggestive of crisp, new bank notes. There was something desperate, almost final in his purposeful movements. I felt a vague sensation of uneasiness.

"Baumann," I remonstrated, "you are not going to do anything stupid, are you? Not suicide? I want to keep my promise to you but I don't want to get involved in anything that might be—er—embarrassing. I am an alien, you know. I'm registered with the Police and an object of suspicion. I'd hate to get into any sort of mess."

He paused in the act of licking the flap of an envelope.

"Suicide? Good heavens, no! But—" he added quickly, "I would like to feel you'd keep your word to me even if anything really drastic did happen. I am not asking you to do something against the law. I'm merely asking you to post a letter for me—to safeguard the happiness of—but, never mind, I know I can trust you."

"Well, what it is you want me to do?" I looked ostentatiously at my watch.

He put into my hands a large, plain envelope. There was no address, no writing on the outside.

"In this envelope," he said, "is another envelope, addressed and stamped. I would prefer that you do not try to find out who it is addressed to, but if your curiosity—"

I shrugged my shoulders.

"All right, then. Now I told you that I may have to leave Cambridge. If I do so, it will be suddenly and at a moment's notice. The method and time of my departure are still doubtful. You will, of course, know that I am gone—if I go. I want you to take this package to the post, open the outer envelope and put the other in the box. If I do not go, I will ask for it back."

"Seems like an awful lot of fuss and mystery. I don't see why—"

"There are reasons," he interrupted, "why I may not be in a position to post it myself. Anything may happen. I may be—er—

incapacitated. I might—" here he paused and seemed to shudder. "I might even be worse than that. But, whatever happens, it is a matter of life and death that this letter should be posted within the shortest possible time of my leaving Cambridge, No, I am perfectly sane," he added, seeing my expression of alarm.

"I'll do it," I said, "and if you ever want the package back and I am not in my room, it will be in the second volume of Boswell's *Life of Johnson*—on the shelf to the right of my fireplace."

A look of relief and gratitude had replaced the sullen expression.

"I don't know how I can ever thank you, Fenton," he muttered. "You've taken a great load off my mind and if there's anything I can do for you in return—"

"There is something," I replied in a tone of assumed indifference. "You could tell me who that girl was who came up here about an hour ago. The one in the raincoat. She went into your room, didn't she?"

While I was speaking I watched his eyes very closely. A hardly perceptible flicker seemed to pass over them but he quickly turned away so that I could not see his face. For a moment I was consumed by an insane, humiliating jealously.

"A girl did some up here some time ago," he replied, and I felt sure that it cost him an effort to control his voice. "She was— she was looking for a John Bowman. I traced him in the registry list for her. He's at Trinity." Not once during this entire speech did his eyes meet mine.

"She told me she was looking for Professor Long," I said suspiciously.

He shrugged his shoulders.

"Perhaps she changed her mind. You know what women are. Sorry I can't tell you more, Fenton, but I don't even know her name. And—thanks a thousand times."

I was late for my lunch with Lloyd Comstock, a nice but rather nondescript youth who occupied a room on the second floor of "A" staircase. He came to fetch me at length and I ran into him just as I was leaving Baumann's rooms. His cheerful face expressed surprise when he saw the direction from which I was coming and he made a few caustic remarks about "My new friend of two and a half terms' standing." Then we went down to lunch.

The rest of the afternoon was peaceful and uneventful. Lloyd Comstock and I played five leisurely sets of tennis and then took a canoe up the Cam to Grantchester. There we bathed and lay naked in the sunshine, talking about nothing whatsoever, reading at intervals, munching biscuits, smoking pipes and enjoying ourselves as only undergraduates know how.

Time seemed to have stood still for awhile and the whole world was bounded by pale blue sky, white scudding clouds and meadows golden with buttercups. There was no shadow to mar the perfection of my happiness.

But, as we paddled back under the college bridges towards evening, the sky had become blotched and angry looking. It was incredibly warm for May. An electric storm was brewing and we felt that we had to race to avoid the rain.

Before going into Hall I procured a students' registry and went through it carefully from Aaronson to Zymovitch. There was no John Bowman at Trinity. There was no Bowman or John Bowman registered at any college in Cambridge. Someone had been misrepresenting facts....

CHAPTER III

Nocturne in "A" Staircase

It is generally believed at Cambridge that the Deity is especially partial to the Latin language and to the classical scholars. At any rate, it is their privilege to address Him at some length in that tongue before sitting down to dinner in the Hall. Those who do not understand Latin must say a Quaker grace in silence, or sit down graceless like Charles Lamb.

On this particular Monday night it was Baumann's turn to pronounce the long blessing. He did it sullenly enough and seemed to be throwing out the sonorous Latin words almost in defiance rather than in gratitude. But he had got no further than *"Oculi omnium in Te sperant, Domine. Tu das iis ..."* when he was interrupted by a terrific burst of thunder.

Everyone was startled, of course, by the unexpected noise, but I noticed that there was an almost terrified expression in Baumann's eyes as he paused and looked apprehensively around him. He seemed completely unnerved and (as Michael Grayling informed me later) actually made a false quantity in the last line of the grace. Which, for a brilliant classical scholar, was almost as startling as the thunderclap itself.

When we at length sat down to our meal, it was to an accompaniment of the pattering of hail. A regular tropical downpour had followed a day that was prematurely summery. I ordered a "college special" for Michael, Comstock and myself to keep the damp out of our bones. No beer in the world ever has or ever will come within nodding distance of the beer known as "college special."

Hall at Cambridge is a compulsory special for at least five out of every seven evenings a week. It is held to be the one time when the whole college collects itself as a body and presents a united front in singleness of purpose and oneness of appetite. It is the nearest approach to our American system of fraternities in that it typifies the principle of forced sociability.

It is the great opportunity to prove or to make oneself a good mixer. It is the undergraduate's daily chance to "meet the men" and to exchange the ideas that they were supposed to have been conning over in their lonely lodgings or crowded lectures. That kindred spirits invariably sit together in little cliques, and that the ideas they discuss seldom go deeper than the carburetors of their respective automobiles or the outcome of the next cricket match, are two points that have undoubtedly escaped the authorities.

Michael, Comstock and I, who formed one of these little cliques, consumed two or three more "college specials," finished our meal and passed outside to join the cluster of undergraduates at the notice boards. The storm—or the beer—seemed to have induced a state of unnatural excitement in all three of us and we decided, with one accord, that work would be out of the question with all this racket going on.

The elements were on the rampage. Nor was it an ordinary polite English thunderstorm with a few sporadic flashes of sheet lightning, but a regular torrent broken by terrific crashes of thunder and lit by jagged forks of flame.

Finally it was decided that we should join forces in my room in half an hour's time.

As I passed alone up "A" staircase, I paused for a moment outside the door of Dr. Warren, senior tutor of the college. He must have left the Combination Room without waiting for his port, for strains of Chopin's Nocturne in E Flat were wailing weakly against the sombre music of the storm. I thought that, if it was he who was playing, I had never heard him play so well before.

As I stood there listening, whilst outside the lightning lit up the exquisite Gothic tracery of the college buildings, I had a moment of rare exultation. I knew this particular nocturne almost by heart, but now I felt I was hearing it for the first time. The delicate appoggiaturas, redolent of roses and Majorca moonlight, seemed to express all the poignant emotions which I had experienced since meeting the Profile that morning; and the dark rumblings of the storm were as an echo of the other tempest which was going on inside me. And all around me was Cambridge— Cambridge omniscient and eternal. In a single day the tempo of my existence had been accelerated. Life was exciting.

We had barely assembled in my room and got a good brew of coffee going when the door opened to admit Mr. Stuart Somerville. We were all a trifle surprised at the condescension and there was an awkward pause.

In the first place the young aristocrat had little in common with the plain, outspoken Comstock; in the second place, we had learnt during Hall that Stuart had once again been picked as twelfth man for the Varsity match that week. His chances for a blue were receding fast and no one knew whether he would like the subject mentioned. The difference between the twelfth and eleventh man is the difference between success and failure. But he was least embarrassed of us all.

"All we need now," he remarked, as he glanced cheerfully around him, "is a chorus composed of Professor Long, the Merry Monocle and Baumann. Hank and the divine Bigger would do as front line comedians. 'A' staircase should all cling together on a night like this. Mind if I join you in a cup of coffee, Fenton on Torts?"

"Delighted, Somerville on Spinach," I replied, smiling. It was impossible to be annoyed for long with the irrepressible Stuart, even when he continued in his best pseudo-Americanized drawl:

"That was a slick little chick I saw you talking to on the stairs this morning. When are you going to introduce me to the girl friend?"

The question was merely rhetorical so I busied myself with the coffee cups and made no reply. I did not know that there had been a witness to the encounter. His agile mind now shifted to a totally different topic.

"You know I wasn't kidding when I told you this morning that North had got out. You'd better cable your old man to have his eye peeled. North escaped last night from the Cambridge Asylum for the Criminally Insane."

"I saw it too," said Comstock casually. "That case was a rum go. An old Saints man, wasn't he?"

"Lived on this staircase—so I've heard," commented Michael.

"See Fenton's Famous Second Trials, Chapter Thirteen, for a full description of the case and increase the coffers of a penniless American millionaire," sang out Stuart. A well-aimed cushion ruffled his blond hair and made him look handsomer than ever.

"Well, it's a fine night for a murderous lunatic to come creeping back to his old haunts," said Comstock, who had a strong leaning toward the sensational.

"Goody-goody, creepy-crawly and spooky-spooky!" cried Somerville. "Let's all tell ghost stories and make a night of it. I've got half a bottle of whisky and some biscuits in my room. Come and help me fetch them, Fenton."

As Somerville and I returned to my room with the whisky, I noticed that Baumann's door was wide open. He was seated at his desk, working. The reading lamp was lit since the storm had made it darker than was usual at that hour. He did not look up as we passed, and his only reply was a grunt when Stuart called out pleasantly, "Congratters on getting on the team, Baumann."

For about half an hour we sat by my window eating cookies and drinking whiskies and sodas while we watched the storm lighting up the battlements of Kings Chapel and throwing into sudden, splendid relief the perpendicular stained windows and the Tudor Roses above the doorway. Never had the familiar spires of Cambridge appeared so fantastic or so exotic. It was a wild, extravagant night.

A plea for ghost stories was again urged, this time by Lloyd Comstock.

"Talking of criminal lunatics," said Michael, after we had drawn the curtains and turned on all the lights, "a queer sort of thing happened last year in the village next to ours. Just a tiny little Gloucestershire hamlet where everybody is either a hundred years old or landed gentry dating back to Edward the Confessor. It was all rather beastly.

"The first thing was that almost every young or youngish woman in the village got an anonymous letter—nasty obscene stuff. I saw one of them because my cousin is married to the village doctor and she got one, too. Somehow or other the writer of that letter had raked up an affair she had had years before with a young captain who was killed in the war.

"The thing had been innocent enough, but insinuations in the letter were perfectly caddish. Even the vicar's daughter, who's no chicken, by the way, got one and almost went potty, she was so upset. The letters were all neatly printed on a kind of old-fashioned parchment. The postmark was Bristol, which is about thirty miles away.

"The police were called in, of course, but they never found a shadow of evidence against anyone. But those letters had brought up more filth than all the dredgers of the Bristol Channel put together.

"Then, just as the excitement was beginning to die down a bit, things took a more gruesome turn. Complaints started to come in that someone was torturing domestic animals. Weird caterwaulings were heard in the dead of night and several cases of horrible mutilations were reported. My cousin's gray Persian kitten was found hanging in an old barn; a prize Sealyham of Lady Standen's had its back legs cut off, and several similar outrages occurred. It was too revolting.

"I was at home at the time and shall never forget the uproar it all caused. I heard of one old farmer who actually took his blue-ribbon sow to bed with him. The RSPCA? sent down a representative and several of the less reputable characters of the community were put under lock and key.

"But the thing went on just the same in spite of the fact that every suspicious person in the place, and every tramp for miles around had a perfect alibi in the local police station. Finally word got about that the perpetrator of all these horrors was not of mortal flesh. A supernatural agency seemed the only possible explanation.

"There was a mound outside the village where an Antichrist was supposed to have been buried in the Middle Ages. Frantic, the villagers flocked to the old vicar and begged him to come to 'lay' the evil spirit. He refused, steadfastly repeating that it was a case for the police and not for the priest. They then approached the young curate, who consented. The evil spirit was exorcised at midnight and a stake driven deep into the ground on the spot where its heart was supposed to lie.

"Next night the ten year old daughter of the village postman was found brutally murdered in a corner of the churchyard. The village was in a state bordering on panic. Of course the thing got into the papers. A Scotland Yard man came down and there was no end of a rumpus.

"Two weeks later the curate was found with his face deeply embedded in the mud of a shallow puddle three miles away. It could not have been a natural death; suicide seemed impossible and there were no traces pointing to murder. I forget what the verdict was.

"From that day on the trouble stopped, and not a soul ever knew who was really responsible. Some say it was all done by the curate himself, others are still confident that no human being could have been capable of perpetrating such horrors. Those were the facts...."

Michael paused and looked around him. There was a long moment of silence.

"Gosh, what a ghastly yarn!" shuddered Comstock, who was an impressionable youth. "You know, somehow or other I can imagine that blighter Baumann being capable of a thing like that."

"Piffle!" I exploded. "If Baumann wanted to kill anyone or anything he'd shoot straight and he'd shoot clean—he'd probably shoot with that revolver Mrs. Bigger is always complaining about. But," I added, "there's nothing the matter with Baumann except that he's homesick, poor devil." These words, coming from an alien, carried a certain amount of weight.

"Of course, Hilary," said Comstock with a slight sneer, "I was forgetting that you and Baumann are friends now."

"We are little friends,
Happy little friends,
We are little friends,
And tutor loves us so—"

chanted Stuart. Neither he nor Michael had ever been heard to say anything against the man who stood between them and what they wanted most in the world. "Have some more whisky, everyone," he continued. "Just a single swallow to make us spring."

"Put a spike in it," I replied, mangling his metaphor and passing the glasses.

"Speaking of village horrors," pursued Lloyd Comstock, when we had all settled down to our drinks, "that was a pretty tragic and weird sort of business when all those women started to die in Crosby-Stourton last summer."

"Hey, you, no family scandal," interrupted Stuart Somerville. "Sir Howard Crosby happens to be a cousin of my governor's and we won't talk about that little tea party if you don't mind."

The argumentative Comstock was about to remonstrate when Stuart continued:

"But if you do want to hear a really creepy yarn I can tell you a story about a fellow I knew at Marlborough. It was a most amazing and uncanny affair...." His voice grew low and serious. "This chap was of a nervous disposition—prone to fainting fits and nosebleeds—you know the type. I got to know him first when we were alone in the school infirmary together—the last victims of an epidemic of some sort—chickenpox, I think, or one of those kiddish complaints. I regarded it as a ripping chance to escape work and slack a bit, but he took it very hard although he wasn't really any iller than I was.

"I remember one night well—it was the night before his birthday and he must have been feverish or something because he begged me to stay awake with him and on no account to let him go to sleep. I can see it now—the long row of white covered beds, the black curtain, the night light flickering in a saucer of water on the mantelpiece, and his pale, frightened face imploring me to talk to him.

"I was sleepy but I promised I'd do my best to keep awake. Then he told me the reason. Ever since he was a kid, he said, he had been subject to a particular dream which was so terrible and frightening that he couldn't even describe it properly. It occurred quite often but he could always count on it the night before his birthday.

"In fact, when he was a kid his parents used to sit up with him on that particular night. They had been awfully upset about it and had taken him to a specialist for treatment. Finally he had found it easiest to pretend he had outgrown his childish fears and to keep the real truth to himself.

"In that sick-room at Marlborough he told me his dream, which, for all his pretended courage, grew more real and more terrifying each year. He dreamt he was in a large dormitory-like room such as they have in hospitals and public schools. There were eighteen beds in the room and he was always sleeping in the end one.

"Suddenly he seemed to be awake, watching the single fluttering gas jet that lighted the room, and *knowing* with that awful nightmare certainty that something fearful was going to happen. Fascinated and unable to turn away his eyes, he would watch the door under the gas light. It used to open very slowly, and then something—something he could not describe—would come into the room.

"It was not a man, it was not an ape, nor a bear nor a wolf, and yet it suggested all of these. With footsteps that were noiseless, yet somehow hideously menacing, it would creep toward one of the beds, and then—then, at that point, he always turned his eyes away, screamed and woke up in an icy sweat.

"But the worst part of the dream was yet to come. In his earliest recollections he never saw the Thing at all distinctly. It always went to one of the cubicles at the end of the dormitory near the door. But each year he seemed to see it more and more distinctly, and this was the worst of all—*every birthday he noticed that it came one bed nearer!*"

Stuart paused a moment and then continued in a more normal tone.

"Well, I did my best to cheer him up that night. We talked far into the early hours of the morning about cricket, the masters, our families, everything on God's earth. Finally, of course, I was so tired that I could hold out no longer. I fell asleep. I was awakened by an agonized scream. The night light had gone out, but I was aware that a figure in white pyjamas was standing by my bed and a voice gasped rather than spoke:

"'It came again, Somerville. I am sixteen to-day and ... *it was only two beds away....*'

"I remember that I jumped out of bed and called the matron. She took his temperature and sent for the doctor. He was frightfully ill next day. Sort of brain fever the matron told me. It lasted for some time and he was finally obliged to leave Marlborough altogether. But—the funny part of it is that I met the fellow two years later. It was just before I came up to the Varsity.

"I was in Switzerland with my pater and stopping in a small inn right up in the mountains. We had just come in from a day's climbing and were feeling frightfully bucked with ourselves. I was drinking Neuchâtel at the so-called bar when suddenly I heard someone say my name. I turned round and found him standing beside me. At first I thought it must be a ghost, he looked so perfectly ghastly!

"'Somerville,' he said, and his face was so pale I could almost see through it like paper. 'Somerville, I shall be eighteen tomorrow. I want to tell you....'"

But Stuart never finished his story for, at this moment the

room was suddenly plunged into complete darkness. A blinding flash of lightning showed us all sitting perfectly rigid in our seats like bodies excavated at Pompeii. There followed a long moment of absolute silence. Then there was a crash.

Whether it was the uncanny tales or the whisky or the storm, I shall never know, but we all seemed to make a rush for the door at the same time. Our nerves had apparently given way in a sort of collective collapse. I fumbled for the light switch, pressed it, but without result. Someone threw open the door. The passage outside was also in total darkness.

I am not at all clear as to what happened immediately, but the next thing I knew for certain was that I was banging against Baumann's sported oak and calling his name.

As I waited for a reply in the awful stillness between thunder claps, I could have sworn I heard a slight movement inside the room and the sound of a match being struck. But perhaps I was mistaken. Cambridge oaks are notoriously thick and I was far from being myself.

"Baumann!" I called again. "The damned lights are on the blink. Can you give me a candle?" There was no answer.

"Better go down and tell the porter," muttered Michael's voice behind me. "The electricity of the storm must have blown out the fuses."

"All right, I'll go," I replied, and started to feel my way down the stairs. When I passed Dr. Warren's rooms there was no light under the door, but as I continued downwards I heard the piano starting to play. This time it was Chopin's *Marche Funèbre,* but I did not stop to listen. Further on, a movement in the gyp's pantry told me that Mrs. Bigger must have been working late. Hank was standing on the ground floor staring out at the rain. He seemed unaware of the trouble on the staircase.

"The lights have all gone out, Hankin," I said.

"Is that so, Mr. Fenton?" he replied calmly. "Well, we can soon fix that up. The porter has the fuses."

We walked over to the porter's lodge together.

"Horl right, sir, horl right," smiled the fat, jovial porter. "Them fuses is busted, I s'pose." I nodded gravely. He turned towards Hank. "I shan't be gone long, Tom, but you'll have to stay here and close them gates at ten o'clock prompt if I ain't back. It's nine fifty-seven now and them gates closes at ten, fuses or no fuses, storm or no storm. Prompt, mind."

Hank nodded laconically. He was quite accustomed to pinch-hitting for the porter just before ten o'clock—the hour at which a heartless Defense of the Realm Act closes the gates of other, more popular, institutions.

The porter trotted off to the infernal regions below his lodge, leaving Hank to play St. Peter. I returned to my own staircase. My eyes were now more accustomed to the darkness but, even so, it was hard to find one's way and there was little or no lightning to help me out. The gyp's pantry was still occupied and Mrs. Bigger's "Goodnight, Mr. Fenton" answered my own. Dr. Warren's piano was still pouring out the saccharine strains of Chopin. There was no other sound except my own footsteps.

Just as I reached the third floor landing, however, I felt rather than heard that there was someone coming down towards me. An uncanny sensation of unreality began to creep over me. It was all like some strange waking dream. As the sounds came nearer, the rustling of a dress became more and more distinct.

There was a woman on "A" staircase—a woman there at ten o'clock at night! It could not be Mrs. Bigger. I had passed her a few seconds before. Who on God's earth could it be? I stood aside, waiting. As I did so, once again there came to my nostrils that faint delicate perfume which I connected so intimately with the Profile.

There was now no mistaking that fragrance. It was so strong that it almost made my head swim. I felt as though I was in the grip of some powerful hallucination.

And then, as I looked towards the passage window, I saw a dark shadow pass in front of it. The shadow of a woman. A sudden faint flash of lightning threw it into momentary relief and I caught a fleeting glimpse of the features whose image had been with me all day. Only a fleeting glimpse.

But it was enough to convince me that the Profile I had just seen must be the same as that which I had seen in the morning. The perfume, too, was the same. For a moment I stood there too dazed to speak. It was all so impossible, so story book, so utterly unacademic. I could hardly believe the evidence of my own senses.

Then a mad resolution seized me. I turned and ran down the stairs after her. I must demand an explanation. But, when I reached the court, I found it completely empty. Once again she had appeared—and disappeared—as if by magic. The pavement outside the gates was empty. No one could possibly have left the college within the last few moments. There was no sound by the chime of the college clock which was just striking the hour.

At the tenth stroke I saw that Hank was solemnly closing the heavy wrought-iron gates.

CHAPTER IV

I Compound a Felony

W HEN I returned to my room I found the whole staircase flooded with light. Lloyd Comstock and Stuart Somerville were nowhere to be seen but Michael was lying on my sofa, smoking a cigarette.

"Gosh, you look pale," he said. "Have you seen a ghost?"

"I'm not at all sure that I haven't," I replied as lightly as I could. "Where are the others?"

"Dunno. When you went down after the fuses they disappeared. Own rooms, I suppose. I stayed here as I wanted to speak to you."

There was a note of seriousness in Michael's voice which I was quick to catch. "Shoot," I murmured abstractedly.

"I had a letter today from my uncle," he said wistfully. "The one that runs a prep school in Clifton. He's offered me a job there next term. I'm afraid I'll have to accept it."

The mania for leaving Cambridge prematurely seemed to be assuming epidemic proportions on "A" staircase.

"But, my dear fellow," I cried impatiently. "You can't possibly give up your chance of getting a degree here. You must finish your third year."

"Can't be done. My pater is dreadfully hard up. The Lenox Scholarship was my only hope and, of course, Baumann will carry that off, damn him."

"How much is the thing worth?"

"Eighty pounds a year. It must sound absurd to you, but to me its the difference between, well—"

I did some rapid calculations. "Why, that's nothing," I said. "I'm not a ruddy millionaire in spite of Somerville's cracks, but I spend that much on 'Gin and Its' every term. Let me lend it to you. You can call it America's contribution toward the depreciated pound sterling."

Michael sat up with a start.

"Good Lord, no," he answered. "I couldn't borrow from you or anyone else. I must carve my own way out. Thanks all the same. It was ripping of you to suggest it."

"Darn your British pride, and darn you, Michael Grayling. Now get this straight. You're not going to accept that pokey little job in your uncle's pokey little prep school. You're not going to leave Cambridge. You're going to win the Lenox Scholarship and you're going to get a first in the Tripos. And right now you are going to promise me that you won't make any decision until after the exam results come out. I have a hunch that one of your chief competitors is going to be—er—eliminated."

"Eliminated?" Michael's voice was pathetically eager. Inwardly I damned Baumann and his arrogant brilliance. This stupid little bit of money meant so much to Michael. It was nothing to the South African except another bauble to satisfy his vanity which was already over-inflated.

And then, Baumann had lied to me that morning. There was no John Bowman at Cambridge at all. He had lied about the Profile. She had been in his rooms before lunch. She had, so I believed, been in his rooms again that night. He must know more about her than he was prepared to admit. He could have saved me from so much mental anguish by telling me the truth, and he could save Michael from disappointment and indecision if he would be more specific about his leaving Cambridge. Why should I not march into his rooms and demand an answer to both questions. And if he refused, then I would give him back his rotten envelope and tell him to go to an even more torrid place than Africa. I was in a fighting mood.

I went over to my bookshelf. The package was still reposing in the second volume of Boswell's *Life of Johnson.* I shoved it angrily in my pocket.

"Wait here a minute, Michael. I'm going in to speak to Baumann." My voice must have sounded strangely purposeful because Michael sat up and stared at me in open-mouthed amazement.

Without another word I strode out, crossed the passage and banged noisily on Baumann's sported oak. There was no sound from his room but a crack of light showed under the door.

"I'll get in if it's the last thing I do," I muttered, still haunted by that fleeting glimpse of the Profile.

I opened the passage window and climbed onto the still dripping roof. Once outside, I walked along the narrow parapet that separated my window from Baumann's. So far it was easy, but as I looked through into my neighbour's lighted room, I almost lost my balance and toppled over backwards into the court four stories below. I had to look twice before I could believe that this was not all some hideous nightmare. I grasped at the window sash to steady myself.

Baumann was stretched face downward on the floor near the writing-table with his head lying in a large pool of blood. Near his right hand I caught the dull gleam of blued steel....

My first instinct was to go back to my own room. It was only the memory of the Profile on the staircase that made me go on. I loved her. If I had ever doubted it before I knew it now as I stood balancing myself outside Baumann's window. I was going to do what I could to help her. For, however innocent her presence may have been—if she had been in Baumann's room that night, she would need my help.

I climbed in through the window. One glance at the body was sufficient to tell that Baumann was dead. He had been shot just above the mouth and the bullet had caused hideous wreckage in his upper jaw. A revolver was lying on the floor close to his hand and half covered also in the blood. The desk chair had fallen over.

On the desk I saw to my amazement that, in addition to an open volume of the *Idylls* of Theocritus and a Greek Lexicon, there was a small tin of the liquid metal polish called Brasso, a cleaning rag and a piece of chamois leather. For a moment I stared uncomprehendingly and then light began to dawn. Every appearance pointed to the fact that Baumann had been cleaning his revolver at the desk when it accidentally went off and shot him in the face. The positions of the body, gun and fallen chair would have forced this conclusion on anyone who had entered the room through the door.

Now, even at the risk of alienating my reader's sympathy, I am going to declare frankly that I never was taken in by all these careful arrangements. As soon as I saw Baumann's dead body through the window, some sixth sense told me that he had been murdered. As soon as I saw the tin of Brasso and the dirty rags I thought to myself, "How clever of somebody. This is a good job. I must keep up the farce." In short, I shamelessly decided to compound what I believed to be a felony. I do not attempt to excuse myself. I can only repeat that I had seen the features of the girl I loved on the staircase that night and I knew that nothing I could do would bring Baumann back to life. If she did kill Baumann, she probably had good reason and I was not going to betray her until I had heard what she had to say for herself. All these thoughts flashed through my head in a very few seconds. Then I suddenly saw, staring me in the face, the most damning piece of evidence in the world—evidence sufficient to prove that what looked like an accidental death was premeditated murder, evidence conclusive enough to send a man to the gallows.

Now the carpet in Baumann's room was light red with a motif of large indeterminate flowers in dark crimson. These were arranged in symmetrical design at regular intervals and there were, of course, spaces in which there was no pattern at all. In one of these spaces, about eighteen inches from Baumann's feet, I noticed that there was a crimson circle which looked, at first glance, like a floating peony or chrysanthemum which had come adrift from its mooring in the carpet's design. I went over and touched it with my hand. It was sticky and my fingers were red. Blood! If Baumann's "accident" had occurred while he was seated at his desk, how could there reasonably be an isolated patch of blood several feet away?

As I stood there trying to puzzle this out, someone banged on the sported oak. Michael's voice cried out:

"Anything up, Hilary?"

"Yes, there's been an accident."

"Let me in for God's sake." His voice sounded tense.

I paused with my hand on the door knob. No. Not even Michael must know my secret. But I must act fast. Now, if ever, was the time for a clear head and rapid thinking.

"Better not," I said as calmly as I could. "Go down to Warren's room and tell him to come up here. It's pretty serious."

As I heard Michael's footsteps retreating, I turned back into the room. Quick, quick, I thought. I must get some alcohol—something to remove that tell-tale second stain. I ran into Baumann's bedroom and the first thing that caught my eye was a queer-shaped bottle of what looked like perfume. *Veldbloemen*, I read on the label, "a distillation of the odoriferous plants that are peculiar to the South African Veld." If I felt any surprise at finding perfume in the bedroom of an athletic Boer farmer, its South African origin explained it. The smells of home are the comfort and the despair of the homesick.

I drenched my handkerchief in the perfume and, as I did so, I felt a dull, sickening sensation in the pit of my stomach. This was the scent which I had smelled when the Profile pulled out her handkerchief that morning. This was the odour which had assailed my nostrils on the staircase. The chain of circumstantial evidence seemed satanically conclusive.

As I rubbed the sinister patch on the carpet with my sodden handkerchief. I could hear the distant sounds of Dr. Warren's piano. Suddenly they stopped. Michael had evidently reached the tutor's rooms. I redoubled my efforts on the stain. The room smelt like a greenhouse. Throwing all the windows wide open, I heard footsteps on the stairs. I stuffed into my pocket the dirty blood-stained handkerchief. There was a soft tap on the still sported oak....

Dr. Reginald Warren, Tutor of All Saints, was not at all the type of man one would expect to play Chopin during a storm. In fact, no one would expect him to play Chopin at all. He tinkled Bach and Mozart occasionally, but first and last he was a scientist—and a rather lugubrious scientist at that. His nickname, the Merry Monocle, was ironical as far as the adjective was concerned, but exact as to the substantive. He had been a colonel in the British Army during the war and had won the V. C. for gallantry on the field. He had never been known to show emotion of any kind whatsoever. If he had passions he kept them to himself or exorcised them with his music.

And his face was quite dispassionate as he stood on the threshold. I saw a look of horror and fear on Michael's countenance.

"Thank you, Mr. Grayling," said Dr. Warren as he adjusted his monocle in his left eye. "I must ask you to return to your room and say nothing. Mr. Fenton, will you please stay here with me?"

He shut the door on Michael. His hands touched the body in various places and then spread in a gesture of finality.

"Mr. Fenton," he said, in the same formal tones I had heard him use in discussing the requirements for Littlego, "he is dead, as you have probably observed. I should say offhand only about twenty minutes, half an hour at the most." He looked at his watch. "It is now ten-fifteen. Did you hear a shot just before ten o'clock?"

"Well, sir," I explained, "there was the storm then and the thunder. Four of us were in my room next door. We heard nothing that we recognized as a shot." I went on to explain about the fuses and my visit to the porter's lodge.

"A curious coincidence," he murmured. "But I suppose it was the sudden darkness that startled Baumann as he was cleaning his revolver. Do you know, by the way, if it belongs to him?"

"I don't know for certain, sir. It was rumoured that Baumann had a gun. The bedmaker has complained."

"It should have been reported immediately," said the tutor severely. "The possession of firearms is strictly forbidden by University regulations." He picked up the tin of Brasso and sniffed at it.

"There is a strange smell here," he remarked. Remembering the handkerchief in my pocket, I instinctively moved away from him.

After a few more questions he said, "Fenton, go to the porter's lodge and call the police station. Ask for Inspector Horrocks. He served with me during the war. A splendid fellow and a personal friend of mine."

"Inspector Horrocks? I know him," I said with relief. "I report to him under the Aliens' Act every time I go down to Cambridge. He's been very decent to me."

"So much the better," he replied drily. "Come back here when you've finished. Horrocks will want to question you, I expect."

Much as I hated to leave Dr. Warren alone with the telltale stain, I departed to do as I was told. After some difficulty I managed to get hold of my old friend Horrocks. My call was transferred from the police station to the asylum, where I just missed getting him. Finally I located him at his home. He promised to come at once and to make arrangements for a police surgeon to follow him.

Inspector Horrocks had always been most affable on the not infrequent occasions when I went through the farcical performance of "registering" as a potentially undesirable alien. Many a beer had we consumed together over a discussion of international problems. But his voice over the telephone sounded so stern and official that I could not believe it was my erstwhile jovial companion.

I reflected that I must dispose of the handkerchief before he arrived on the scene. My hand furtively sought my coat pocket and, as it did so, it came into contact with the letter Bauman had given me that morning.

This set me thinking. Having done all I could to prevent the avenging of the South African's death, I felt that the least I could do was to comply with the last request he had made me. Perhaps I was rattled, perhaps I was over-conscientious, but in the excitement of the moment I did something that I was to regret many times later. I pulled the letter from my pocket, tore open the outer envelope and placed the enclosure in the letter box near the lodge. I did not look at the address, but as the envelope fell down the slot, I caught the letters B-R-I-D-G-E-S. Then I saw the porter look inquiringly towards me. I moved quickly away, but not before I had noticed that the outer envelope, which I still held in my hand, was blood-stained from its proximity to my handkerchief.

Here was another piece of evidence to destroy. Well, there is a classical place to dispose of useless paper; and if paper, why not a handkerchief also?

Nodding goodnight to the porter, I strolled casually towards the one corner of the college where one can go without question at any hour of the day or night. There I tore the envelope and the handkerchief into small pieces and safely dispatched them on their long journey down the Cambridge sewer pipes.

I breathed a sigh of relief and lit a cigarette in a vain attempt to hide the fact that I still smelled like a lady's boudoir. Then I washed my hands and returned slowly and thoughtfully to the room where Baumann's body lay.

It was not until I saw him still lying there, under the cool scrutiny of Dr. Warren, that I reflected that Michael Grayling's problems were undoubtedly solved, and that Stuart Somerville would now get his much-coveted cricket blue. It was indeed an ill wind that had blown that night, but it could not fail to bring some good to my friends on "A" staircase.

CHAPTER V

I Wrestle with Authority

INSPECTOR HORROCKS of the Cambridge Police always made me doubt that the war was really over. Though I had never seen him in any kind of uniform, I felt that he belonged in the drawings of Bruce Bairnsfather—at least he was the type of Englishman which that eminent cartoonist tried in vain to caricature. But no mere pencil could ever give adequate expression to that plum-and-apple complexion, those guileless china blue eyes or that red walrus moustache. It would require the brush of a Raeburn or a Reynolds to do justice to Inspector Horrocks' peculiarly English type of—well, not exactly beauty. He was the final epitome of much beef and beer; the glorious, solid result of plain living, military discipline, and no hanky-panky when it came to high thinking.

But Inspector Horrocks was also a man of infinite resource and sagacity. If, during our not infrequent visits to the "Plumed Cock," I had underestimated his mental powers, I very soon revised my opinion when he finally reached Baumann's room at eleven o'clock that Monday night.

"Well, sir," he said, turning deferentially to Dr. Warren, who had been explaining his theory of the accident, "if he was cleaning his gun when it went off in his hand there'll be powder marks on his face to show it was point-blank range, as you might say, sir."

Dr. Warren lifted up the mangled head without speaking. Indeed, words were unnecessary, for no powder marks or anything else could be seen on that terrible, blood-stained countenance.

"Then there's the bullet, sir. It usually goes right through in such cases. We ought to find it somewhere in the room."

"I thought of that," replied Dr. Warren, "but the bullet didn't pierce the skull. You can see for yourself there's no hole in the back of the head. Strange," he mused, "the cerebrum is as soft as putty. The bullet must have been deflected on passing through one of the frontal bones. Now if it had been a spent bullet, we might have expected—" His voice trailed off.

Horrocks picked up the revolver and wrapped it in a large pocket handkerchief. As he did so I stole a furtive glance at the isolated blood stain and noticed, to my relief, that it was now almost invisible. "It's no good even trying to get fingerprints off this gun," he said in disgust. "I never did see such a mess. Worse than Dunkirk, eh, Colonel?"

The two old soldiers smiled gravely at each other and, as they did so, I noticed that Horrocks' eyes looked at Dr. Warren with an almost doglike devotion and admiration. I suspected then, as I afterwards found out to be the truth, that it was by saving Inspector Horrocks' life that Colonel (then Captain) Warren had won his V. C. Our tutor could do no wrong in the eyes of Cambridge Law as embodied in Inspector Herbert Horrocks.

After he had washed his hands and taken a careful survey of the room, Horrocks produced his notebook and began to question me. There was hardly any need to be untruthful. No, I could not say that I had definitely heard the shot. Nor had I seen or heard any stranger go into Baumann's rooms. I knew of no circumstances which should make the South African wish to take his own life. Yes, I had some reason to believe that the gun was his own, and, as Dr. Warren suggested, the sudden extinction of the lights might well have startled him and caused the pistol to go off. It had certainly startled me. When I came to think of it, there had been a crash about that time but, of course, we had all taken it for thunder.

One question, however, was not so easy.

"If you didn't hear the shot, Mr. Fenton, what made you climb over the roof to get into his room that way?"

I paused before replying.

"I wanted to speak to Baumann. I knew he was in since there was a light under his door. I banged and banged. There was no answer. So finally—"

"I didn't know Baumann was such a close friend of yours," interrupted the tutor, looking at me narrowly.

"Well, sir, we were neighbours," I commented lamely.

"But even with neighbours, surely, one respects the sported oak."

Before I had time to reply, Horrocks suddenly made a dive towards the fireplace.

"See here, sir," he said, holding up a partially consumed match. "Here's a match."

There was indeed no doubt about it. Its significance, however, was not immediately apparent to us two victims of higher education.

"Well," explained the inspector, stating the fact as though it was the most obvious thing in the world, "the deceased young gentleman didn't smoke. Not an ashtray in sight. Not a packet of gaspers, as you might say, sir; and—what's more—not a match neither. Not even in his pockets."

Here was deduction indeed. Dr. Warren and I were flatteringly impressed.

"And what is one's first instinct when lights go out?" continued Horrocks sagely. "Why to strike a match, of course. And if Mr. Baumann hadn't got a match, well, it may mean there was someone else here who *had.*"

This was terrible. I could almost feel the colour come and go in my cheeks.

"Perhaps I can explain that," I stammered out at length. "I smoked a cigarette in here this morning while I was—er—having a little chat with Baumann. You can see the end of it in the fireplace now. Probably that was the match I used to light it."

Horrocks' little balloon of triumph seemed to have been summarily pricked. He looked almost crestfallen, but I thought I saw a flicker of relief pass over the tutor's mask-like countenance. After Horrocks had asked a few more questions and received generally satisfactory answers, Dr. Warren gravely summed up his own conclusions.

"I am quite satisfied myself, Horrocks, that this was a case of accidental death. At present I see no reason to suspect otherwise. The position of the body, the wound and the revolver all seem perfectly reasonable to me. Indeed, I sincerely hope that such will be proved the case. One point, however, I feel I ought to mention. When I entered this room I had a distinct impression that a woman had been here. There was a strong smell of perfume."

The word "woman" alarmed me so much that I completely lost my head and burst forth into a tissue of half-lies.

"I think I can explain that, too, sir," I said in a voice so calm that I was surprised at my own duplicity. "When I saw Baumann lying there, I didn't realize at first that he was dead. I ran into the bedroom to see if I could find anything to help him. While I was there I upset a bottle of perfume that was on his dressing table and got it all over my sleeve."

"Perfume?" The tone was sceptical.

I went into the bedroom and produced the bottle. Dr. Warren sniffed at it and peered through his monocle.

"Well," he said, "that's certainly the odour I smelled."

The arrival of the police surgeon put a stop to all further inquiries that were not strictly medical. Dr. Warren counted the title M. D. amongst his other academic distinctions, and could talk to the medical examiner in his own language. Polysyllabic words such as intercranial pressure, cerebral hemorrhage, medulla oblongata and corpus striatum were tossed lightly to and fro like so many ping-pong balls. Horrocks and I indulged in a lay conversation on the side.

Finally Dr. Warren turned to me and said, "I think, Mr. Fenton, I must ask you to come with me while I report this matter to the Master. He has guests at the Lodge tonight, but I'm afraid we shall have to trouble him." He turned to Horrocks. "Will you find your way over there when Dr.—er—Beaverly has made the necessary arrangements?" The inspector nodded.

Whatever the truth about our Master, the longevity of the Cambridge don is notorious. The excellence of the college cellar is probably responsible, on the principle that the better the preservative the longer the preservation.

Dr. Hyssop, the Master of All Saints College, was as warm and human as Dr. Warren was austere and formal. We could hear his benevolent voice booming out goodnights to his guests as we stood on the porch waiting to be admitted. The door opened at length and we saw the fine leonine head (he justifiably prided himself on his resemblance to his old friend, George Meredith), the snow-white beard and kindly, tranquil eyes. Dr. Warren and I stood aside for his guests to pass, and I scrutinized the ladies carefully in the wild hope that the Profile might be among them or that I should see some young woman whom I might have mistaken for her on the staircase that night. No, they were all middle-aged or elderly and there was not a soul there, man or woman, that I did not know by sight; each of the ladies was as far beyond my suspicions as Caesar's wife herself or the Master's only surviving granddaughter, who was acting as hostess.

After the party had dispersed, Dr. Hyssop turned to give me one of his famous electric handshakes.

"Well, Hilary, my boy," he said warmly. "This is indeed a pleasure. And how is my old friend, Aloysius Fenton? Is he still championing the cause of the desolate and the oppressed on the bench of the Supreme Court?"

I told him hastily that my father was well. As I smiled into that kindly face I felt instinctively that I wanted to put off the bad news about Baumann as long as possible. Dr. Warren had no such scruples, however, and as soon as we had seated ourselves in the Master's comfortable study, he launched forth into an account of the South African's death.

While he was talking I forgot for a moment the enigma of Baumann. My eyes wandered round the fascinating room. It was warm and personal as the character of its owner. Its untidiness and haphazard arrangement gave it a charm of its own; periods and personalities were inextricably blended in a glorious hodgepodge. There was a signed portrait of Lord Tennyson (next to one of Bernard Shaw), another of Thomas Hardy, affectionately inscribed "To Mart from Tom." A very recent Matisse hung on a William Morris wallpaper; a bust of Meredith adorned one corner of the room; in the other was Rodin's famous head of Dr. Hyssop himself. The mantelpiece was full of photographs. These I examined with interest; and I caught the face of my father, looking absurdly youthful and unimportant despite his court robes.

The sight of him brought me back with a start to the unfortunate present. Dr. Warren had finished his tale, and the Master was making clucking noises like a distressed hen. It hurt me to see the pain which we had involuntarily inflicted on this benevolent old gentleman.

"Poor boy!" he murmured, "how sad, how very sad, how very sad! I don't recall ever meeting him. What year did you say he was in, Warren?"

"He's a second year man, Master. Plays cricket for the University and looks—or rather, looked—certain to get his blue this year. He was a good classical scholar, too. Came to us from the University of Grahamstown on a sixty pound open scholarship—a South African of Dutch extraction. Well-to-do people, I imagine. By nature he was morose and anti-social. Disliked college activities and had few friends. A most unpopular fellow with the other undergraduates."

I was amazed to learn that, despite all appearances to the contrary, each hair of our heads is numbered by the authorities.

"Dear, dear," sighed the Master. "It will mean an investigation, I suppose. The police, the coroner—all that kind of thing. I shall leave it to you, Warren. I just can't wrestle with it." The faded eyes lost their light for a moment and looked infinitely weary. "It will do the college no good, I'm afraid. But we shall survive it, just as we survived that sad affair of William North. Dear me, dear me!" The Master passed a hand over his face as if to wipe out a painful memory.

And indeed the story of William North, though it had sounded humorous enough when referred to by Somerville that morning, was one of the most tragic incidents in the history of the college. William North had been one of the most brilliant French students of his day; his book *Rabelais et Son Siècle* was (and for all I know, still is) the last word on an intricate and hitherto little appreciated period in French literature. The young author had once had the academic world at his feet. It was even predicted that he would one day have his picture hung in the College Hall along with the other immortals. Today it was blazoned on the front page of every newspaper in England.

As an undergraduate, and before all his troubles started, North had made an unfortunate marriage with a local barmaid. The marriage was doubtless perpetrated in a moment of Rabelaisian impetuosity. It had not, however, hindered him from getting his fellowship at All Saints and his lectures were reputed to have been among the most brilliant ever given at Cambridge.

He lived with his wife and two children, happily enough, at Madingley. Every vacation he would rush off to France, where he explored the Rabelais country around Chinon, always seeking for fresh material to put in his ever growing volume. He was a terrific worker and a prodigious scholar.

And then, almost immediately following the publication of his book, the crash came. For some time he had been nervous and irritable; overwork during a neglected attack of influenza had induced a mild form of brain fever. He attended his classes as usual. One day the most horrible screams were heard issuing from his rooms on "A" staircase (those now occupied by the staid Dr. Long).

The oak was sported; the screams died to a hideous, strangled gurgling. When finally the door was opened, a madman was discovered gloating in sixteenth century French over the dead body of one of his most brilliant woman students. The corpse was hideously mutilated. There was talk of an outrage of an even more terrible nature.

William North was tried and condemned to death. The case completely eclipsed for a time the notorius Crippen trial, with which it was almost contemporaneous. A clever counsel got the case appealed on a legal technicality. Then followed the second trial of William North, which was so interesting in the legal points involved that my father included an account of it in his *Famous Second Trials.* My father happened to be present at both the trials of North and saw his sentence commuted from death on the gallows to confinement for life in the Cambridgeshire asylum for the criminally insane.

That this confinement had now come to an abrupt termination was the theme of Inspector Horrocks, who had joined us in the courtyard after we had said goodnight to the Master.

"It's a strange thing, Colonel," he said, biting the ends of his enormous moustache, "that the two things should have happened almost in one day as you might say, sir, and both of them involving this college of yours. I've been working all day on the North case and a rare job I'm having of it, trying to trace his footsteps, though every police station in the country has been wired a description of him. I was thinking sir," here his voice dropped to a confidential whisper, "that if Mr. Baumann's death *wasn't* accidental—well, there was murder on 'A' staircase once before, and they say that murderers always return to the scene of their crime."

Dr. Warren gave a little start, and his eyeglass fell from his eye. His face was pale in the moonlight.

"Nonsense, Horrocks," he exclaimed. "Your imagination is running away with you. North was a scholar and a gentleman. His—er—unfortunate lapse occurred twenty years ago whilst he was very ill and his mind temporarily deranged. You know as well as I do that fundamentally he was not a criminal—and incidentally he was one of my greatest friends."

The inspector mumbled an apology. "Well, I must say, sir, he's been quiet enough and docile like in the 'home' there. Was allowed to do almost anything he liked, as you might say, sir. Given the run of the establishment almost. No one dreamed as how he was lying in wait for his opportunity to get away. All the staff was surprised and hurt, sir—surprised and hurt. The superintendent felt it was casting reflections on his treatment as you might say."

We had now reached "A" staircase. I was thinking how little inclination I felt to go up to my own room, past Baumann's door.

"Have you finished in *there?*" asked the tutor, with an upward jerk of his head.

"Yes, sir," replied Horrocks. "The body has been removed. Dr. Beaverly agreed with you as to the time of death, sir, and we have found nothing else of a suspicious nature. It will be 'Death by Misadventure' all right, Colonel."

"So much the better," said Dr. Warren. "Good night, Horrocks."

"Good night, Colonel, sir. Good night, Mr. Fenton. I shall have to trouble you again tomorrow, I'm afraid. I hope the coroner can arrange to sit on the case by Wednesday or Thursday. Good night."

Dr. Warren and I parted at the door of his rooms. As I paused a moment I heard again the soft notes of his piano. A look of annoyance passed over his face and he wished me an abrupt good night.

Someone was in Dr. Warren's rooms—someone who did not know or did not care that musical instruments are forbidden after 11 p.m. And whoever was there played Chopin much better than Dr. Warren did—and very differently. There was a certain abandon, a divine delirium never achieved by our tutor in his sporadic tinklings.

But I was too tired to worry my head about these further

complications, so I ran upstairs as quickly as I could and went straight to bed. When sleep finally came, I dreamed a dream strangely similar to that of Somerville's unfortunate Marlborough friend. I was in bed in a strange room which suddenly seemed to become more and more familiar.

Eventually I realized that it was Baumann's, but instead of being a sitting-room it was now a dormitory full of beds, all empty except the one I was in, and one other. Outside, it seemed, a thunderstorm was raging. Then slowly the door opened and a figure entered.

It advanced toward the other occupied bed. I could neither move nor cry out. The figure glided onwards. I closed my eyes, and when I opened them I noticed that the occupant of the other bed was now lying face downwards in a position which I knew only too well. Beneath the head was a dark, growing stain.

The figure was now retreating towards the door, but before disappearing it half turned towards me. It was the Profile. She was speaking—speaking to me in a clear, yet somewhat unearthly voice, and across that strange yet familiar room I heard her repeating the marvelous words of that macabre poem by William Blake:

> O Rose, thou art sick!
> The invisible worm
> That flies in the night
> In the howling storm,
>
> Has found out thy bed
> Of crimson joy;
> And his dark secret love
> Does thy life destroy.

CHAPTER VI

Two for Lunch

I awoke next morning with what can only be described as an emotional hangover. My mouth felt dry and fuzzy, and I had the uneasy sensation of a thousand wrong things done. The outlook was overcast, meteorologically and spiritually. The only coherent thought in my head was that I must see the Profile today and help her if possible.

As I took a deep draught of tepid water from my ewer, a delicate "Ahem" came from my sitting room. It was Mrs. Bigger. She had been on the staircase last night. Perhaps she had heard or seen something. I must question her without arousing suspicion.

"Proceed, Sherlock," I muttered, lighting a cigarette with a kind of haggard nonchalance.

One glance at my good bedmaker showed me that she was near to bursting point with suppressed ideas. How long she had been waiting for me to wake I cannot tell, but my room had never been so tidy before in its life. This was my first intimation that I had become a Personality.

"Mr. Fenton," hemmed Mrs. Bigger, "I didn't like to slop you up while you was a-sleepin', sir, 'cos I reckoned you must be tired, seein' as 'ow it was you what discovered 'im, sir"—here her voice dropped to a gruesome whisper—"lyin' stark and rude in nothin' but 'is own blood, as I heard this mornin' from that there gentleman as was asking for you, Mr. Fenton."

I yawned ostentatiously.

"Has someone been looking for me, Mrs. Bigger?" I asked. The ostrich plumes nodded in affirmation.

"Yes, sir. A man with a big red moustache, and 'e said 'e'd be back again later and not to disturb you just now. Her tone implied that it might well be the last undisturbed sleep I should have for a very long white.

In answer to the implication of her words, therefore, I gave her a bowdlerized version of my last night's excursion over the roof and the finding of my neighbour's dead body. When I had finished, she pronounced gravely:

"It don't do to speak hill of the dead, Mr. Fenton, but I 'ad told Mr. 'Ankin that Mr. Baumann didn't ever hort to of been allowed to 'ave a pistol in 'is room, sir. I seed it there wiv me own eyes, Mr. Fenton, but—and this shows the meaness of 'im—he always kep' it in 'is—ahem—biscuit tin there on the mantel shelf. And when Mr. 'Ankin told 'im I'd complained, Mr. Baumann said, 'So Mrs. Bigger was after my biscuits, was she?' So you see I didn't have no legs to stand on. But I knew the pistol was there, sir, biscuits or no biscuits. And I wasn't the only one as knew it either."

"You'll probably have to identify the gun at the inquest," I remarked, and her eyes brightened. "Perhaps you can give some more evidence, too. You were working here pretty late, weren't you? You didn't hear the shot by any chance, I suppose, or—er— see anything out of the ordinary?"

For a moment I found myself hanging on Mrs. Bigger's lips as though she were a young girl to whom I had just proposed. The reply, when it did come, was reassuring, if a trifle discursive.

"I didn't 'ear nothing, Mr. Fenton, and as for seein', well, with the lights out that way I couldn't 'ave seen me 'and a hinch from me nose. I'd been 'elping over at the Master's lodge till almost ten o'clock, sir, 'cos Mary Smith was alone and there was company to dinner. She'd never have got them things washed if it 'adn't been for me and I'd asked 'er to come round to my 'ouse afterwards, Mr. Fenton, seein' as Tuesday is 'er day out, sir.

"I was waitin' for 'er in the pantry when the lights went out and I didn't 'ear nor see nothin' 'cept you when you called out good night and once a noise outside Mr. Somerville's door, sir. And then, soon after the lights went on again, Mary was waitin' for me and all I remember is that I said to 'er, jokin' like, 'Mary, 'as someone just kissed you? 'Cos you look blinkin' 'appy,' and she blushed and looked pretty, sir, 'cos there was Mr. Hankin standin' there by her side and I thought how they two was a-courtin', sir, and well—you know wot young people is in the dark, sir, when no one's lookin', as it were. And then Mrs. Fancher from 'C' joined us and Mr. 'Ankin let us all out the gates and we went round and 'ad a dog's nose at Fancher's, sir, 'e being a publican and we 'is wife's friends—"

I cut her short. There was no shadow of doubt as to her movements on the previous evening.

"Mrs. Bigger," I exclaimed, "What in heaven's name is a dog's nose? It sounds perfectly excellent. I feel I could do with one right now."

"Well, Mr. Fenton, it's a mixture of stout and gin. You mix—" But here Mrs. Bigger paused, her face suffused with a maidenly blush.

We were treading on dangerous ground, and skirting the fringes of a dreadful secret which my bedmaker had, in an expansive moment, confided to me some time previously. She had once been a barmaid. In fact that had been her occupation when the late-lamented Bigger had first spied her ample charms and finally transferred them to his undertaking establishment off Chesterton Road.

Mr. Bigger had joined his own coffins long since ("sarcophagus in the throat, Mr. Fenton, and crool 'e suffered"); but had Mrs. Bigger slid back into the perilous paths of bar-maidenhood? No, a thousand times no. Whenever she returned to the taps she kept on the customer's side of the counter, just as when she made beds she kept on the right side of the blanket.

There was evidently nothing of real importance to be learned from Mrs. Bigger, and I was not altogether sorry when a deputation consisting of Lloyd Comstock, Michael Grayling, and Stuart Somerville caused her to beat a modest retreat. My three "stairmates," with the possible exception of Comstock, all looked rather the worse for wear this morning. There was an expression on Michael's face that amounted almost to antagonism and a film of reticence over Stuart's usually frank blue eyes. I attributed this to the fact that both of them were likely to benefit through Baumann's death and they would naturally feel some embarrassment about squeezing their feet into the shoes of one so recently dead.

Lloyd Comstock, however, pressed me for details in a perfectly normal and ingenuous manner. All three of them had already been interviewed by Horrocks and another detective that morning, and not one of them had, as far as I could ascertain, contributed any facts of new or startling interest. The words "murder" or "suicide" were not mentioned, and it was obvious that they looked to me for sensationalism, if there was any to be had. I intended to disappoint them, nursing my guilty secret like a mother with a sick baby.

So far, so good. My next visitor was Horrocks, who brought with him a long, cadaverous individual whom he introduced as Sergeant Rollings. Horrocks, smartly dressed, carried a small suitcase in his hand.

"Mr. Fenton," he explained apologetically, "I've been called away to London on the North case. Last night all indications pointed to the fact that North was still somewhere in Cambridge. This morning he's supposed to have been seen in London. It may be a false alarm, but I've got to go. Sergeant Rollings will take care of this Baumann business in my absence. I'm sure you will help him all you can." We nodded gravely at each other. He continued:

"If all goes well—and I see no reason why it shouldn't—they will hold the inquest on Thursday. You will have to appear, of course." We nodded again and then Horrocks took his leave.

I accompanied Rollings into Baumann's room and once again

went through the performance of discovering the body for his benefit. His questions were, for the most part, neither intelligent nor pertinent. My only strong emotion in the whole business was a hope that he would not make me late for lunch with the Profile.

At twelve o'clock, however, he departed and I returned to my room to shave, change my tie, and make the best of my rather limited store of natural attractions. I regarded myself critically in the spotted mirror. A poor face, but mine own, and rather worse than usual, I reflected. Not that I am an Adonis at the best of times.

I can however, boast a set of decent teeth, curly hair, and not one single pimple. Let us be thankful for small mercies.

But I was not so thankful as I should have been that morning as I sallied forth to my optimistic lunch party. I wanted to be a superman to match a superprofile.

On the way to meet her at the "Whim" I reflected that, often as I had heard Baumann's name mentioned, there had been no word of regret from anyone. It is possible that his tutor would miss him as "the only person in Cambridge capable of appreciating at once the spirit and the text of Pindar," and the Varsity cricket captain would sigh for that famous cut past second slip which was to have played such havoc with the Oxford bowlers.

But other scholars would come up next term, and other batsmen would take his place on the team. Kindly is our fostering mother, kindly but fickle.

When I reached the "Whim," a fine drizzle was moistening the pavements. Instinctively I looked around for the Profile's mackintosh. There was no sign of it or her; only a sprinkling of elegantly dressed young men absorbing an excess of carbohydrates and all talking. Even as I entered I heard the words, "discovered by a chap called Fenton, an American." Like Lord Byron I had awakened to find that I had become famous overnight.

In another corner of the room a girl sat by herself avidly reading a newspaper account of the accident. One glance showed me that her profile was anything but the one I was looking for. I must sit down and wait. I did so. Half an hour passed and no sign of her. I had had no breakfast. Even people in love must eat. I was torn between my desire for food and my longing to see her again—to hear her tell me that there was nothing—

"Excuse me, but are you by any chance Mr. Hilary Fenton?" The girl from the far corner had come across the room. In her hand she held a letter—my letter. Then she must be bringing me news of the Profile. A thousand awful possibilities flashed through my head. She had been killed—arrested—she had run away—she needed me—

"Yes, my name is Fenton," I replied eagerly.

The girl simpered for a moment and then looked coyly downward.

"Well, I got your letter," she giggled, "I'm Dorothy Dupuis!"

Hell, damnation and all the Furies—it was the prominent girl in spectacles who had been sitting next to the Profile at the lecture. Confound those attendance lists. Confound the Profile. Confound Lady Snorting Lusinger. Confound everyone.

"Oh—h, so nice of you to come," I smiled weakly.

"Well," she replied primly, "it was rather a sketchy invite. I ought not to have done it but Lady Lusinger *is* my aunt, so I suppose it was all right. And then I was curious—feminine, I suppose—to see in the flesh the person who discovered the body. I read about it in the papers this morning and called up my fiancé to ask if he minded my lunching with you. He's an undergrad at Cats—reading theology, you know."

I didn't know, nor did I care. And I loathe the abbreviation *undergrad.*

"Well, what about some food," I suggested hungrily. As we waited for our orders to be served, Dorothy Dupuis bombarded me with questions concerning Baumann, Lady Lusinger, the depression in America and my church membership. Even my appetite had left me by now. I felt cheated and furious with the Profile, but alas! more in love with her than ever. Great is the power of contrast.

When we got to the horrible English concoction known by the frivolous title of "Trifle," I decided that I would combine the cunning of the serpent with the softness of the dove. This luncheon should not be wholly wasted.

"Who was that girl you were sitting next to at the Blake lecture?" I asked as casually as I could. "And have some more trifle, won't you?"

"Yes, ta, you mean the one in the mac—" (the girl had a positive genius for odious abbreviations) "or Jean Higginbotham?"

"Oh, no, her name couldn't possibly be Higginbotham," I cried fervently.

The thick lenses were flashed on me suspiciously, but I parried her unspoken thought. "If you're a friend of hers, why don't you tell her to buy a new raincoat. The one she wears is the limit. Is she very poor or something?"

"Heavens, no! Camilla Lathrop is as rich as Croesus. But her father is in the clothes business, so I suppose she thinks it's too much of an advertisement to dress well. You know Lathrop and Lathrop of Bristol. Besides Camilla affects to despise men, but I think she only does it to make herself more mysterious and intriguing."

(Apparently the theological fiancé was not the only link which this young lady had with Cats!)

"But why are you so interested?"

"I thought I saw her last night," I replied indifferently, "somewhere around ten o'clock."

"It's quite poss. We all went to a debate in Sidney on the subject of 'Woman in Politics.' It ended at nine forty-five punc. Camilla didn't speak though I'd asked her to second me. She is always so unpredictable. In fact she was down in the papers to be presented at Court this year, then flatly refused to meet their majesties. Just as if they weren't good enough for her—" Here she gave a snort that was worthy of her august aunt. "Ridic, I call it. All this posing as a blue stocking and turning up one's nose at society and men and dances and other things. When all's said and done a woman's a woman and—"

At this juncture the complement of her womanhood appeared on the scene wearing a St. Catherine's blazer and a rather vacuous smile which was meant to be jealous, ferocious and protective all at once.

"Oh, Perce, this is Mr. Fenton of Saints. A great friend of my aunt, Lady Lusinger." Miss Dupuis removed what I am sure she would have called her "specs" and wiped them.

My hand was seized in a clammy, lifeless clasp. I murmured polite banalities and finally surrendered Lady Lusinger's niece to her budding bishop. Then I went on my lonely celibate way, reflecting sadly that there are approximately four hundred women students in Cambridge to about five thousand males.

What chance was there for me with a girl like Camilla Lathrop, especially when she didn't much care for my sex in general, and didn't care enough for me in particular to rescue me from the ghastly mistake I had made through a foolish misinterpretation of the attendance list?

I was rather depressed. My lunch had got me nowhere at all, unless it was a place in the bad graces of Miss Dupuis. True, I knew the Profile's name at last, but I did not know whether she had been on the staircase last night. Her feline friend had not established an alibi for her. I must do some detecting on my own account.

A brilliant idea struck me. I purchased a small handbag and unblushingly fitted it with lipstick, powder and a few coins of the realm. Armed with this feminine paraphernalia, I approached the Porter's Lodge, where Hank and the porter were engaged in conversation on the all-engrossing subject of Baumann.

"I picked this up at the foot of 'A' last night, Porter," I said casually. "Just after I had told you about the fuses. Has anyone been enquiring for it? I should say it belonged to a *young* lady, judging by its cosmetic contents."

The porter took it in his hand and peered inside.

"You can't tell these days," the porter said gloomily.

"Well, were there any young ladies in the college last night who might have dropped it?"

The porter turned to Hank.

"No, Mr. Fenton," replied the gyp, "there was no ladies went through the gate while I was on duty."

"It must have been dropped around ten o'clock," I insisted mildly. "Didn't any women leave around that time?"

"No, sir," replied Hank, "leastways there weren't no ladies, sir. There was a bunch of bedmakers and the maid from the Master's lodge—" here a faint blush tinged Hank's countenance. "They left shortly after ten, sir. But that bag wouldn't belong to none of them. That's a real expensive bag, sir."

"Then there was the Master's lady guests," continued the porter reminiscently, "but it couldn't of been any of them. They left around eleven in a body, sir, and they didn't go near 'A' staircase. I saw them walk across the lawn with me own eyes, Mr. Fenton. Right across the lawn they walked and them not fellows."

"Oh, all right, keep the bag and see if anyone claims it," I said airily. "And be discreet, Hankin. You're a lady's man yourself, you know—and—"

But Hankin was now blushing so violently that I did not finish my sentence. Instead I winked knowingly at the porter and departed to my own room.

Detective Fenton, I reflected, had established at least one fact by this little subterfuge. If the Profile was in All Saints last night she had managed to get out without being seen. There is one and only one exit to a Cambridge college at night time, and that is through the main gateway past the vigilant eye of the porter or his subsidiary.

It could safely be presumed that my dark and mysterious lady was not a cat burglar who could climb over spiked fences twenty feet high or slide down drain pipes like the members of the Cambridge Alpine Club.

But even for the Alpine Club this was a tough proposition. All Saints had this much in common with Heaven—it was almost impossible of entrance by unauthorized persons at unseasonable hours. And as for getting out—well, to keep up my simile, it was as difficult as Hell.

And I know, because I have tried both.

CHAPTER VII

Kind Hearts and Coroners

THE REST of Tuesday and all of Wednesday were a complete blank so far as really interesting developments were concerned. In the first place I had hardly a moment to myself. The publicity given me by the newspapers quickly brought every American in Cambridge to call on me, and whenever I sought security behind my sported oak, Sergeant Rollings, would come and bang on it and ask me a lot more foolish questions. And Comstock, who hovered around me all the time, was no help; he took a malicious delight in showing me off to all and sundry.

Michael Grayling and Stuart Somerville kept out of my way. The one was doing a last hour rush of work for the examination on Thursday and the other spent all of Tuesday practicing at "the nets," whatever they were. And on Wednesday the match against the M. C. C. started. Stuart had been given Baumann's place on the Varsity team and was grimly determined to deserve his vicarious laurels.

Each day I scanned the papers for news of the recapture of William North. Apparently he was still at large. So far Horrocks' trip to London had not been successful.

Once or twice I ventured out into the streets, and once I went to a lecture in the vain hope of seeing the Profile. She seemed to have gone out of my life as mysteriously as she had come. The idea persisted, however, that I should see her at the inquest, which I had been summoned to attend on Thursday at 2:30PM.

But I was doomed to disappointment, for when I reached the coroner's court she was nowhere to be seen. The newly returned Inspector Horrocks was chatting informally with Dr. Warren as I entered.

The small room seemed running over with people and, despite the fact that there was a Varsity match in progress at Fenners, I noticed a fairly large proportion of undergraduates. A shudder passed through me as I reflected how that shrouded form in the back room was one of the undergraduates who ought now to be engrossed in cricket rather than in this gruesome game of death.

A roll was called, and a number of rather seedy-looking individuals segregated themselves with little smirks of self-importance. These were the jurors. I watched the simple proceedings, fascinated. Though I am the son of a judge, I have always been very vague about courtroom ceremonies and coroners' inquests in particular. In fact, I had rather imagined that in England they were endowed with the pomp and ceremony—the wigs and robes—of a murder trial at the Old Bailey. But this was almost as informal as a breakfast party with the Dean.

The coroner, a sleek man of middle age, reminded me of a croupier at Monte Carlo. When he gave a little rap with his gavel and announced, "I declare this court open in the King's name," it was as if he had cried, *"Faites vos jeux, messieurs et 'dames."*

The wheel of the inquest had now started to spin. The jurors were asked if they had viewed the body. They nodded. The witnesses were then called. Aloysius Hilarion Fenton—

I flatter myself that for a normally truthful young man I gave my evidence in the calm, cool manner of an accomplished prevaricator. There was, however, no occasion for me to tell a direct lie. What I should have done if the temptation had arisen, I cannot say.

As it was, I merely described how I had banged on Baumann's door and, receiving no answer, had climbed in by the roof. I went on to tell about the position of the body and the cleaning materials.

I repeated for the hundredth time that I was not a close friend of the deceased. I knew of no reason why he should wish to commit suicide and certainly knew of no one who might wish to take the South African's life. The coroner thanked me for my evidence as though I had just put a hundred-franc note in the croupier's box.

He then gave the wheel another turn and produced Inspector Horrocks. His evidence dealt chiefly with the fingerprints, or rather the lack of fingerprints, on the pistol. He was soon followed by Dr. Warren, who did little besides corroborating my testimony. The tutor added a brief summary of Baumann's position in the college, his enviable record in South Africa. The jurors looked slightly bored.

Dr. Beaverly was much more interesting. He described almost dramatically how he had been sent for at about ten-thirty pm on Monday night to examine the dead body of a young man about twenty-four years old. Death had been caused by a bullet from a .32 calibre revolver which had entered the head in the region of the superior maxilla, been deflected by one of the frontal bones and finally lodged in the cerebrum, whence it had been extracted at the autopsy.

Death had not been instantaneous—but must have occurred very shortly. This, he opined, probably accounted for the fact that the revolver lay by the side of the dead man and was not clasped in his hand.

Here the coroner interrupted with what seemed to be a very sensible question: "Would you say that the shot was fired at point-blank range, Doctor Beaverly? If so, were there any powder marks on the face of the deceased?"

The police doctor hesitated a moment. Finally he said, "In my opinion, the bullet was fired at very close range. There were no discoverable powder marks, however, since the skin around the wound became obscured by clotted blood. If, however, the gun had been fired at a distance of two or three inches, as might have happened in the case of suicide, there would be traces of burnt skin around the wound. Such traces were not found, and it is my opinion that the pistol was at least a foot away from the deceased's face when it was discharged."

At this point one of the jurors, who was obviously a medical man, asked whether it was significant that the bullet had lodged in the head without passing through the skull, as might have been expected.

Dr. Beaverly looked very judicial when this question was propounded. "Of course," he finally elucidated, "the cerebrum and the medulla are well known to be very soft. In seven cases out of ten a bullet fired at close range will pass right through the cranium, but in some instances, when deflected by a bone, it follows the course of the bone and finally drops downward.

"That, in my opinion, is what happened in this present case. I do not think that we must necessarily argue that the bullet was fired from some distance on this account. A few yards or a few inches make very little difference; the bullet might have acted as it did if fired from anywhere in the room."

Everyone seemed completely satisfied and I noticed that Dr. Warren regarded the police surgeon with cold approval.

The next witness was a complete stranger. He gave his name as Johann Van der Walt, lawyer, and head of the London branch of the South African law firm who had handled Baumann's affairs. His evidence dealt with the family life and financial status of Julius Baumann.

The deceased, he explained, was the adopted son of Heinrich Baumann (bachelor), deceased, of Bloemfontein, Orange Free State. When he came of age, Julius had inherited ten thousand morgen of farm land in the Orange Free State, and several thousand pounds in cash. Now that he was dead the property reverted automatically to a nephew of the late Heinrich Baumann, also of the Orange Free State.

The money, however, over which Julius had complete control, could have been willed in any way the deceased wished. In this connection the lawyer added that the young man had withdrawn money fairly heavily of late and only about eighteen hundred pounds remained to his credit. This would normally have been supplemented in due course by revenue from the farm.

Mr. Van der Walt was not prepared to say what Julius had done with the sums he had withdrawn lately, though he had every reason to believe that he had a considerable amount of cash by him at the time of his death. The estate would be settled as soon as it was definitely established that the deceased had left no will.

Sergeant Rollings was called next and gave some routine information with regard to the revolver found by Baumann's side. It was made by Hinder and Dapp, of Cape Town, and carried a .32 calibre bullet such as had been extracted from the dead man's brain. Nor, indeed, was there any doubt as to its ownership since the name Julius Baumann had been engraved on the handle.

A search through the dead man's personal belongings had revealed nothing of any significance.

There was no more testimony to be called.

The coroner looked amiably around him, twiddled his thumbs, and then rose to make his summing up. *"Rien ne va plus."* ... The jury was whisked off to consider the verdict and returned in a very few minutes with the only possible decision according to the evidence presented—Death by Misadventure.

No one was surprised. Indeed, everyone seemed quite gratified. I was delighted at my own success at compounding a felony without any deliberate lies. I passed out into the May sunshine, cocksure that I had put something over.

But Nemesis was stalking close behind, and caught up to me soon after I reached my own room.

As I threw myself down on the couch, I began to take stock of my position. I had kept faith with Baumann by posting his letter and saying nothing about it. I had stood by the Profile in destroying any evidence that there had been a second party in my neighbour's room on Monday night; I had followed the line of least resistance at the inquest. But my conscience kept telling me that the Law is not mocked for long. I was restless and uneasy.

Then as though it were the echo of my own uneasiness, I heard sounds in the room which had lately belonged to the ill-starred South African. Someone was moving the heavy trunks and boxes which I had noticed yesterday by the doorway—the trunks that contained Baumann's personal effects—the trunks which were now all packed and corded, ready to be sent to Mr. Van der Walt in London.

Curiosity impelled me to go and see who was there. Through the half-open door I caught a glimpse of a broad man's back bending over the largest packing cases. As I entered the room, Inspector Horrocks straightened himself and mopped his brow with a large purple handkerchief.

There was an expression on his face which made me think of a naughty little boy who had been caught stealing apples. In his hand he held a recently disinterred bundle which looked as if it could do with a wash.

"Looking for the missing link, Inspector?" I asked with every appearance of innocent unconcern.

The detective shut the trunk slowly and deliberately.

"Mr. Fenton," he said without smiling, "I'd like a word with you—a word in confidence like you might say, sir."

"All right. Come into my room. I've got two bottles of Guinness. We need a pick-me-up. I've also got some gin so you can fix yourself a dog's nose if you like."

"Guinness is mine," he replied, and again the purple handkerchief was passed over the florid countenance.

Clasping the bundle beneath one arm, he followed me into my room. There was an uncomfortable sensation in my bones that a noose was being slowly but surely tightened.

The inspector cleared his throat. "Mr. Fenton," he remarked, as he laid his bundle on the table, "I'm in what you might call an awkward predicament, sir. I thought perhaps I could talk to you as man to man—"

"Shoot," I murmured, inwardly cursing those previous sessions at the Plumed Cock and the inverted snobbishness which had made me so anxious to be "buddies" with a police inspector.

"You see, sir," he continued, "the coroner is satisfied as to the cause of Mr. Baumann's death, but I can't honestly say that I am. And that's where the awkwardness of it comes in, Mr. Fenton. As you know, it was not, strictly speaking, my case. I only came into it to oblige Colonel Warren, as you might say, Mr. Fenton."

"What on earth do you mean, Horrocks?" I asked, filling up his glass with a none too steady hand. "Have there been any fresh developments?"

The inspector took a long pull at his stout, taking meticulous care not to get any froth in his moustache.

"No, sir, nothing fresh. Only the things that would have been obvious to any man in the world except Sergeant Rollings. That man, Mr. Fenton—" he tapped his broad forehead with a significant gesture, "—of course, this is all confidential and would be very bad for the Cambridge force if it got out, but what with me being called to London after North on a fool's errand and Dr. Warren having saved my life—well, you see my position, sir."

His incoherence positively took my breath away. "No, I'm afraid I don't," I answered, "but I have half a dozen more Guinnesses in the cupboard if that's any help. And why not fill your pipe?"

I pushed a crested tobacco-box towards him and fetched two more bottles. When Inspector Horrocks had made himself comfortable on the sofa he said in a voice whose quietness accentuated the gravity of his words:

"I think, Mr. Fenton, you appreciate my position better than you are prepared to admit. I think you know in your heart of hearts, that Baumann was murdered in cold blood, and murdered by one of the cleverest and luckiest criminals that you or I ever came across. Isn't that the truth?"

At home in America I had been told by speculators that, when they lost everything they owned in the Stock Market collapse, their first feeling was one of relief. I did not believe them at the time. Now I understand what they meant. In trampling down my carefully raised structure of half-falsehoods, Horrocks had taken from my mind a terrific load of responsibility.

"So you are a psychologist as well as a detective, Horrocks," I said, lighting a cigarette with exaggerated insouciance. "But I really think that before you go any further you ought to substantiate such a very damning remark. You haven't by any chance got a warrant for my arrest—as an accessory after the fact?"

"No, sir," he smiled, "I know you didn't have anything to do with it. I was watching you all through the inquest and I think you were telling the truth. The only trouble is you weren't telling *all* the truth. I'd only just got back from London so I didn't have time to work out your reasons for acting as you did. I know there are a great many things that are puzzling you, too. Perhaps we can help each other."

"You are talking through your hat, Horrocks," I cried. My voice, however, sounded thin and far away.

Horrocks gave me a comfortable smile. "Now, Mr. Fenton, as the son of a judge and being, like you might say, older and more experienced than the average undergraduate here, I can surely ask you to listen to reason. The thing is as plain as the nose on your face, begging your pardon, sir. When I first came in on Monday night I was prepared to accept things at their face value. But while I was in London hunting for William North, I suddenly got to thinking about young Baumann, how he was a cricketer and a South African and how he was probably a good shot too. They live by the gun out there, I understand—"

"But what on earth—?" I interrupted.

"Just a minute, just a minute, Mr. Fenton," he continued. "If you'd lived with firearms as long as I have, you'd realize that ten o'clock at night is the worst possible time to clean them. You can't even see down the barrel properly. And then, if Mr. Baumann was used to firearms, he would never have started out to clean his pistol without first removing the bullets. In the middle of a thunderstorm, too. The thing just doesn't fit."

He looked at me quizzically and reached out a hand for his glass. It was empty. Mechanically I filled it.

"But, hasn't it struck you, Horrocks, that you might easily be working up an excellent case for a rather deliberately planned suicide?"

The inspector spread out his hands in the hopeless gesture of schoolmasters faced by wilful stupidity of their pupils.

"I thought I had explained to you," he said patiently, "that Mr. Baumann was born with a gun in his pocket as you might say, sir. Well, if he wanted to make his suicide look like an accident, he would hardly have left on his desk materials that are never used to clean guns or revolvers. When all's said and done, Mr. Baumann had some brains."

"But I don't follow you, Horrocks," I cried, now really mystified. "There *were* cleaning materials on the desk!"

Horrocks shook his head. "Brasso is used to clean brass buttons and not gun-metal or blued steel. I wonder the colonel didn't tumble to it himself."

This appeared to make excellent sense. I stared in undisguised admiration.

"I have just established two further facts, Mr. Fenton," he continued quietly. "Facts that I should have established long before the inquest if I had not been called away like that. In the first place there was nothing made of brass in Mr. Baumann's possession—nothing on which he might reasonably have used Brasso. I have also found the materials which he *did* use when he wanted to clean his revolver." He pointed to the dirty bundle on the table. "They were in the bottom of a trunk and I'd say they have not been used for some months, but they are the kind of things a real shooting man might use and not be ashamed of, sir."

The man was obviously headed for a high place in Scotland Yard.

"Now look Mr. Fenton. Here's my own revolver." He whipped it from his pocket. "And here's a tin of Brasso. See what happens when I try to clean it."

He sprinkled some Brasso on the gun-metal and rubbed it with his handkerchief. A nasty gray smudge was the result.

"*Demonstratio ad oculos,* and very conclusive, Mr. Holmes."

"Then you agree with me that the tin of Brasso and the chamois leather were deliberately *planted*, Mr. Fenton? Planted by a clever murderer, but one who was not clever enough to find out the first thing about cleaning guns?"

"But how on earth did he know where Baumann kept his revolver?" I asked.

"I don't imagine Mrs. Bigger was very backward in coming forward about a thing of that sort, sir. You know what women are when they have a grievance. She knew herself where it was kept and probably broadcast the news around like you might say, Mr. Fenton."

"Well, your murderer had a lot of luck," I commented briefly." The storm to drown the noise of the shot. The blood to hide the fingerprints. You'd have a job to convince a jury, Inspector."

"You may call it luck, but I think it was mostly good management, Mr. Fenton. And then, there are some more facts to come out, sir. You are not the only one who is keeping information to himself. There are other people on this staircase, sir."

"Well, it's a good thing you are not relying on what I can tell you, because I assure you that my knowledge won't get you far.

"My only suggestion is that you find out from the porter who came in or left the college around ten o'clock on Monday. If it really was murder, it was probably an outside job."

"I've already done that, sir." He produced a dirty piece of paper from his pocket and passed it on to me. It was a list of the exits and entrances on Monday night. Before ten o'clock there was no record of importance.

After ten there was the mention of numerous undergraduates, a few college servants and the Master's guests. After twelve there was one entry only—"Dr. Warren and friend." I should love to have known the sex of that "friend."

"Why do you show all this to me?" I asked suspiciously.

"Well, Mr. Fenton, my position is awkward, sir. Any disclosures now would discredit Sergeant Rollings and besides, if the Coroner is satisfied, the matter should really be closed. But I am convinced that Julius Baumann was foully murdered. I hoped," he added simply, "you might be interested in helping me to prove it."

It was obvious that he disliked as much as I did the conclusions which his intelligence had forced upon him.

"Horrocks," I said, "I want above all things in the world to find out who murdered Baumann. I will do everything I can to help you—under two conditions. The first is that you trust me sufficiently to let me keep to myself the things that concern me only—" he nodded without smiling—"and the second is that you tell Dr. Warren what you have just told me and let him know that you intend to continue your investigation in spite of the coroner."

"It will break his heart," he murmured sadly.

"Nonsense, Horrocks. Now, finish up your stout and I'll go down with you right now. Courage, my friend—the devil is dead, but we'll find out who killed him."

Reluctantly Horrocks followed me down to Dr. Warren's rooms. There he told the story which he had just imparted to me. Dr. Warren listened to him in silence, staring at his fingernails through his monocle and fidgeting occasionally with his feet. It was obvious that he wished his old friend Horrocks in Jericho.

"So you see, Colonel," finished the inspector, "as soon as I've traced North, I can turn my attention to this case and work on it myself. Tactfully like you might say, sir. I hate to reopen old wounds, but I did feel it my duty ..."

"Of course it's your duty," snapped the tutor. "Facts are facts and we have to face them. I think we've been very lucky with our coroner's verdict. Now no one need know that you suspect foul play. Mr. Fenton, you will be discreet, of course."

"I've promised the inspector to help all I can, sir," I replied, "and I shall, of course, keep it to myself."

"Good. Then you have my full permission to go ahead, Horrocks. I can trust you to keep it out of the papers."

"You can indeed, sir, and thank you. It will be a great thing for my reputation on the force if—"

"And a great thing for the reputation of the college," said the tutor, grimly. "Still, a duty is a duty, even if it is an unpleasant one."

We realized that we were dismissed.

As I shook hands with Horrocks outside, I felt that the clasp sealed a pact. I was glad, at last, to have the Law on my side.

When I returned to my room, I was surprised to see that someone was standing by my bookcase, casually pulling out a volume. My visitor was a girl wearing a red hat and a smartly cut white silk dress. As I entered the room, she wheeled round and faced me. It was the Profile....

CHAPTER VIII

Purple Patch

I HAVE already mentioned the fact that nice English girls do not run around loose in the men's colleges at Cambridge. This applies most especially to the women students at Girton and Newnham.

Meters of red tape must be unraveled before they can accept an innocent invitation to tea. If they come uninvited, they are flying in the face of all the standard conventions and acting as hussies. The statement is unqualified—and yet, here it was, time for tea or cocktails, and the Profile was in my room, uninvited!

"Hullo," she said calmly, as I entered. And indeed, she did look rather a hussy in that flaming red hat and the stunning white dress. But an exquisite and perfectly adorable hussy at that. Whatever poise or good breeding I have acquired at the two Cambridges completely deserted me as I took in the miracle of this sudden re-appearance.

"Where in the name of all that's wonderful do you come from?" I asked fatuously.

"Fenners. The M. C. C. is all out at last for three hundred and eighty-six. I'm afraid the Varsity hasn't a chance. Cricket, by the way, is almost my only vice—if you exclude an occasional cigarette."

I passed her my case in a dazed manner.

"Thanks. I do hope you don't think this is cheek of me, but I wanted to see you. I feel I owe you an apology, Hilary Fention."

"Several, Miss Lathrop." The memory of that lunch at the "Whim" still rankled.

"Come, it's not so bad as all that," she smiled. "But, I am glad you've got my name right at last. I only heard today about your tête-à-tête with Dorothy Dupuis. She told me all the 'circs' during the match this afternoon. I've been laughing ever since."

"It's almost as funny," I said sulkily, "as when an old lady slips on a piece of orange peel in the street and breaks her leg."

Her face grew serious for a moment. "Please don't be cross," she said. "You can't blame me for not being the person you thought I was. You got the girl you invited and she's really a very good sort, if a trifle earnest. There's nothing wrong with her except that theological fiasco. I thought, in common charity, it would be amusing for her to have a change from him. You must admit I'd have been a cat—and a rather conceited one—if I'd taken it all to myself and done her out of what you call a 'date' for lunch."

"All right," I said. "I'll forgive you if you'll stay and have tea with me now. I have three rather stale cakes, a box of chocolate biscuits and some Graham crackers. We can make toast."

"I'd love to. I'm dying for tea after all that cricket. And you are going to let me help, aren't you?"

She removed the red hat and started to busy herself with the loaf of bread and the teapot. The late afternoon was growing a trifle chilly, so I put a match to the fire. We chatted gaily and inconsequentially as we prepared our informal meal. It was all very pleasant and cozy but, somehow or other, each of us seemed to know that the other was acting a part—that we were both marking time before a stampede of inevitable questions and answers.

It was not till after she had poured out my third cup of tea and urged me to take the pink marzipan cake before it went completely bad, that she broached the subject which was uppermost in both our minds.

"Hilary Fention," she said suddenly, "have you forgotten that you saw me on this staircase last Monday morning?"

"You know perfectly well I haven't forgotten. How could I?" I moved out of my chair and sat beside her on the couch.

"I hoped you had," she said softly.

"Oh, I see what you mean. Well, as far as that goes, I haven't told anyone about it—nor about that other time. But naturally I am curious."

She looked at me for a moment as though she were trying to make up her mind about something. Then she said with a lift of one eyebrow:

"And what are you curious about, Hilary Fenton?"

I drew a deep breath. Now or never, I thought, and both feet are better than one.

"Well, it all boils down to this, Camilla. I should like to know whether or not it was you who murdered Baumann."

"*Murdered—*" She sprang from her seat and stared at me with wild and startled eyes. For one second she stood there speechless and then, gradually, every trace of colour disappeared from her face. Her knees seemed to sag beneath her and, almost before I had had time to realize what was happening, she had fallen back on to the sofa in a lifeless little heap.

And as I saw her lying there, looking so small and defenseless on my enormous, overstuffed Chesterfield, I suddenly lost all control of myself.

"Camilla, Camilla darling," I burbled, as I chafed her cold hands between my own, "don't take it to heart, dear. What does it matter even if you did do it? I don't care. No one need ever know. Just open your eyes and tell me that you forgive me."

Then, I am ashamed to say, at a moment when reason dictated

that I should have emptied the contents of the water bottle on her, I started to kiss her eyes, her hair, her forehead. And I probably said more foolish things in those few seconds than in the twenty-four years of my life which preceded them. Her very frailty seemed to enhance her loveliness. It was a moment of delirium.

But, like all the great moments of my life, it was destined to be cut short. The next thing I knew the little hand, which I had lately held so tenderly, was landing a stinging smack on my face.

"Ouch!" I cried, stepping quickly away from the prematurely recovered Camilla, who was now sitting up and glaring at me ferociously.

"I'm ashamed of you, Hilary Fenton," she said, half laughing, half crying. "First of all you call me a murderess and then you start to maul me like a—like a tiger. And my hair's a mess and I haven't a comb, and—and, oh Lord—where is your chivalry and your mirror?"

I rubbed my stinging cheek. "Chivalry, my dear Camilla, is a mere bluff invented by men to hide the shallowness of women. You'll find a mirror and a comb in my bedroom there."

But she did not move. Instead she pulled out her pocket handkerchief and started to cry. She didn't do it as well as the girls in the movies but it was quite a creditable effort. Neither her eyes nor her nose became unduly red or shiny. Perhaps she sniffed a bit too much, but that was doubtless due to the sincerity of her feelings.

"Oh, what a nasty great hoyden I am!" she gasped. "To come into a young man's rooms uninvited and then smack his face. I'll never forgive myself—never—and, oh, Hilary Fenton, there's a purple patch on your cheek."

"Purple patch!" I replied with some heat. "The whole darned thing is like a purple patch in some penny novelette. It's all too utterly—too incredibly fantastic!"

"Well, it's no good *my* trying to be dramatic about anything when I look as though I'd just been pulled backwards through a haystack in the floods. Wait a minute."

She jumped up from the couch and disappeared into my bedroom. When she returned, the ravages of the last few minutes had been repaired and an April smile played about her lips. But there was still tragedy in her eyes.

"Now, I feel better," she cried, "and if you'll give me a cigarette, I'll sit still as a mouse whilst you tell me why you accuse me of

all the seven deadly sins and breaking all the commandments."
Here her voice grew more serious. "Incidentally, I am particularly
interested in the sixth. Whom am I supposed to have murdered?"
"Camilla," I said gravely, "do let us be frank with each other.
This is no time for fooling, pleasant though our dalliance be." My
hand again sought my burning cheek. "You came here today either
because you wanted to tell me something important or because
you wanted me to tell you something. You've made it very obvious
that you didn't come for the sake of my *beaux yeux.*"

"But they are rather beaux," she murmured. Bless her!

"Now listen." Then I launched forth into the whole story,
beginning at the moment when I found Baumann in my room on
Monday morning and ending with her unexpected presence that
afternoon. I omitted nothing—not even the part about Baumann's
letter.

It was only when I described my seeing her silhouette on the
stairs that a puzzled frown passed over her forehead. For the
rest of the time her face was emotionless as one of the Elgin
marbles.

Even after I had finished she continued to look straight in
front of her. When she did turn towards me, her eyes were shining
and her voice was very low. "And you did all this for me, Hilary
Fenton, without even knowing who I was.

"It's the most wonderful—well, I can't use long words—but to
think that I dared to talk to you about chivalry and then—slap
your face!" Here she looked at me with a strange, enigmatic smile.
"But much as I appreciate all you've done, I must tell you quite
frankly that I was nowhere near your college on Monday night. I
was at a horrible debate in Sidney."

"But, Camilla, it must have been you. I know your profile better
than I know my own mother's. And then, that perfume. I'm
frightfully sensitive to perfumes—I'd know that one anywhere
and, God knows, I hate it now."

"Listen," she said slowly. "I can explain everything. At least, I
believe I can. Even the vision on the stairs. You saw me at the
lecture. For some reason or other my face struck you as funny—
or something. No—don't interrupt. You met me and, being keen
on nice smells, you naturally noticed that perfectly lovely *Flowers
of the Veld* which I've used for some time now. (Ask any of my
friends in Newnham. They are all crazy to know its name and
where I get it.) Well, to resume. My image was on your mind.
You'd been telling ghost stories. The lights had gone out suddenly.

You had, I'm afraid, been drinking too much whisky. At any rate you were all strung up and someone passed you on the stairs. Probably it was just another undergraduate but you imagined it was me. It's quite obvious what happened, and I think I understand the rest, too."

"Well, that's more than I do. I'll admit, if you like, that the chances are against it's being a woman that I saw Monday night. If it was, she either disappeared into thin air or slid down a drain pipe. Maybe my imagination *was* overheated with regard to the face, but the perfume was real. That I'll swear to."

"I don't think so—at least, unless the person you saw had taken it from Baumann's room. Now, I'm going to tell you something in exchange for your frankness. Something I never meant to tell anyone. I did know Julius Baumann slightly. No, there was absolutely nothing between us. I didn't even like him much.

"I met him first two terms ago. We had friends in common. It was then that he gave me some of his wonderful South African scent. I liked it so much that I ordered a bottle from the *Parfumerie Française* in Rose Crescent. They said they never sold it and would have to get it all the way from South Africa. Finally I got it and it cost a small fortune but it was worth it.

"I never saw Julius Baumann again until last Monday morning. If you don't mind, I'd rather not tell you exactly why I went to his rooms, but one of his friends was in trouble. He was the only person who could help. That's why I am so thankful—yes, and so grateful—to know that you posted his letter and that you never told. I really came here this afternoon because I thought you might be a friend of Baumann's and that you would know something—"

"But, Camilla," I interrupted, "Inspector Horrocks knows that Baumann was murdered. He is investigating the case and he seems like a jolly good detective. It may be dangerous for you to keep things to yourself."

"If I thought for one single minute that any knowledge I have would help find out who killed him, I would gladly and willingly tell," she said simply. "As it is, it would do more harm than good and make me and several other perfectly innocent people very unhappy. You must continue to take me on trust—up to a certain point.

"But one thing is definite. I did not kill Baumann. I was nowhere near his room that night. I hadn't the remotest idea that it was anything but an unfortunate accident. The word murder was an awful shock. That's why I made such an ass of myself by fainting or whatever it was I did.

"But if ever I do learn anything that might be useful, I will tell you immediately. The only suggestion I have at present is that you ask at the perfume shop whether anyone else has bought *Veldbloemen*. That might be a help. In the meantime could you go on forgetting that you ever saw me on the staircase at all?

"And could you forget that vision—which you saw later on in the evening? Could you do that for me, Hilary?"

She was now putting on her red hat and making ready to go. I could see that she was deeply moved by all that I had told her and evidently could not trust herself to talk much more.

"I'd forget anything in the world for you, Camilla," I replied quietly, "everything except the fact that I love you."

She took a step towards me and looked at me so long and searchingly that my head began to swim.

"You are a dear," she whispered at length, "a perfect dear, and I wish I loved you, too. But girls don't go quite as fast as all that, I'm afraid. However—" Here she bent suddenly forward and her lips brushed the place on my cheek where her hand had slapped me—"Now we are quits, aren't we? And—friends?"

I smiled. "Okay, pal. But don't be a sister to me. I've got three already. And when do I see you again?"

"Well, you know I never can resist cricket. I'll be watching the Varsity match tomorrow afternoon."

"Oh, Lord," I groaned, "we certainly *are* friends if I have to endure the horrid mysteries of cricket for you!"

She laughed happily. "I wish you knew how sweet you look, Hilary Fenton, when you are sulky and disgruntled that way. And I wish you knew how lovely it is for me when you stop treating me like a woman of mystery or a kind of poisonous lotus. And you'll go on that way, won't you, please? You'll treat me just as though I was another man or, at the worst, a simple, uncomplicated English girl who works eight hours a day and minds her own business?"

She had now reached the doorway.

"That'll be all right by me, buddy," I called after her retreating figure. "But if you wear that damned mackintosh tomorrow, I'll—"

But she never heard the completion of the threat, for, with a swift valedictory smile, she had disappeared down the staircase.

I looked at my watch. It was five minutes to six o'clock, which left me no time to dwell on my emotions if I wanted to get round to the *Parfumerie Française* before they closed. I dashed towards Rose Crescent. There I found that the misty blonde who presided was just about to call it a day.

"Good evening" I said politely. "Do you happen to have some perfume called *Veldbloemen?* It's South African, I believe." I wrote the name down for her on a slip of paper.

"Oh, yes. *Flowers of the Veld,* as it's called. I haven't any in stock but I can get some for you," she said. "Our London dealer can obtain it. Of course we don't get many calls for it and it's rather dear."

"Some people buy it though, surely?" I said naively.

"Why, yes, occasionally. I remember that a young lady bought some here last October. A nice-looking young lady—a most refined face. And then, this term it was, a young man ordered some most particular and then made quite a fuss about the price when he got it. I explained to him that with the duty—"

"Was he an undergraduate?" I asked.

The woman looked doubtful for a moment. "I don't hardly know, sir. He was older than the usual run of undergraduates, and his voice was a bit funny."

"No one else?"

"No, sir, that was all. Can I order some for you, sir?"

"What's that? Oh, no. I think I'll take something simple, uncomplicated and English. How about a shilling bottle of Yardley's lavender?"

As she wrapped it up for me, I reflected that Camilla's suggestion had not got me much further. The two people who had bought *Flowers of the Veld* were just the two that one would have expected—Camilla Lathrop herself and Julius Baumann.

There seemed to be no possible doubt as to that.

CHAPTER IX

I Sharpen My Pencil

FROM THE days of my earliest adolescence I have set my face against the profession in which my father has become such a distinguished luminary. That is to say, I have opposed it as a career for myself, preferring to believe that I was headed in a vague way towards the diplomatic or consular service. And yet, of necessity I have acquired some smattering of law in the home circle and occasionally my father pops out in me when least expected. My actions are seldom judicious, but I flatter myself that sometimes my mind takes a turn that is surprisingly judicial.

That evening, after Hall, was one of the times in question. I had received the Aristotelian purgation through pity and terror; I had run through the whole gamut of emotions during the day. Now that the night was coming, I felt Olympian and aloof; I was ready to weigh, with sublime impartiality, the pros and cons of the Baumann case.

I went to my room, rolled up my sleeves and proceeded, literally and metaphorically, to sharpen my pencil. And very sharp I made it. Would I could have sharpened my wits to that same fine point.

First of all I decided to draw up the facts of the case, going on the assumption that the South African was—as Horrocks implicitly believed, and as my own reason told me must be the truth—deliberately and cold-bloodedly murdered. This being assumed, I went on, in a somewhat haphazard manner, to write as follows:

1. Baumann was killed between 9:45 and 10:05 P. M. with, perhaps, a variation of five minutes each way.

2. The lights went out at approximately 9:54 P. M. It is possible that the murderer was in the room at this time, but by no means certain. He could have got out just before the stampede from my room or even earlier. I was not inclined to attach too much importance to the fact that I thought I had heard a match strike when I knocked at Baumann's door to ask for a candle.

3. My neighbour's door was wide open when I went down with Somerville to fetch the whisky earlier in the evening. Unless he shut it later on, the murderer could have entered the room without trouble.

4. If Baumann had sported his oak, Hank was the only person who could have got in through the door since he alone had a key to the outer door.

5. Anyone, however, could have got into the room through the window in exactly the same manner as I had done when I discovered the body.

6. Obviously the murderer knew that Baumann kept his revolver in the biscuit box on the mantelpiece. Although Mrs. Bigger had been anything but reticent about the hiding place, it did point to the fact that the field was limited to an inside agency—if not to the "A" staircase itself.

7. The murderer was undoubtedly a remarkably intelligent person. Indeed, if he worked in the dark, as was more than possible, his care—or his luck—was almost superhuman.

8. And as a corollary to number seven: If he worked in the dark, even with the aid of a flashlight, he must have been intimate with the geography of the room.

9. Another indication that it was an inside job was the fact that no stranger was seen to leave or enter the college just before or just after the closing of the gates.

10. Baumann obviously expected trouble of some sort. Though, if Camilla was to be believed, the trouble in question would have no bearing on his death. His open door also pointed to the fact that he neither anticipated nor feared any kind of personal violence.

This brought me up with a jerk. There are almost 5,000 undergraduates at the University, any one of whom might have borne the South African some sort of grudge. There are about 59,262 regular inhabitants of Cambridge and some 39,067,000 people in England and Wales, any one of whom *might* ... No, the complexity of the situation made my brain reel.

I must stick to the possibilities of which I knew something. I must confine myself to the people who could reasonably and logically have committed the murder. In short, I must go on the assumption that it really was an inside job, otherwise I might just as well break the point of my pencil, tear up my notes and go jump in the Trinity Fountain.

I proceeded with my wholesale prosecution as follows:

The Case against Hankin

Hank was the only person who could have got into Baumann's room if the oak had been sported since he alone had the keys to the outer doors of each room on "A" staircase. There was no doubt as to his presence at the time of Baumann's death since I myself saw him when I went down to report the fusing of the lights.

That brought up another point which had not yet been established one way or the other. Had the fuses been destroyed by the electricity of the storm, or had someone deliberately plunged the staircase into darkness in order to consummate the murder without being recognized?

In the latter instance no one (except possibly the porter) could have tampered with the electric system more easily than Hank. On the other hand, Hank above all others was the one person to whom darkness would not be an asset, since his presence in any room on "A" staircase would at no time be suspicious.

Another point against our gyp was the fact that he was the only person, to my knowledge, with whom Baumann had ever achieved anything that approached intimacy. Indeed, he was the only person who might be supposed to know anything at all about the enigmatic South African. Hank also came from South Africa and a glance at the atlas showed me that his native town of Kroonstad was not far from Bloemfontein where the Baumann farm was situated. Perhaps there was some dark secret in my neighbour's South African past to which Hank alone held the key.

And this brought up another point. Hank had been very nervous and jumpy since Baumann's death. Usually he was rather a phlegmatic young man who took his job seriously and minded his own business. Lately, however, I had noticed that a flush came into his cheeks at any mention of Monday night. On two occasions he had neglected to empty my ashtrays—a terrible oversight on the part of a college servant.

But if he had borne a grudge against Baumann, it was only logical to suppose that the latter had been unaware of it, since he had asked the gyp to witness his signature on the document which I had posted for him.

Then again, Hankin cleaned Baumann's room every day with or without the aid of Mrs. Bigger. He would be able to find his way about in the darkness as easily as by daylight. He knew exactly where the revolver was kept. Indeed, he had not reported its presence in the biscuit box even though he must have known that it was there against regulations.

In short, Hankin had the means and he had the opportunity. Perhaps the motive was to be found somewhere in the dark continent—somewhere in the obscure mist of their heterogeneous pasts. At the present time, at least, it was not visible on "A" staircase.

The Case against Dr. Warren

As far as I knew, Dr. Warren had been in his room on "A" staircase all Monday evening. He could at any time have gone to Baumann's room and gained immediate entry in his official capacity as senior tutor. His scientific knowledge would have helped him to conceal the traces of his guilt. His eagerness for the "accident" theory was all too transparent and it might even be classed as suspicious that he summoned to investigate the case the one man who was under a deep obligation to him. His manner, too, had been strange on Monday night—more cold and harsh than usual—and the misplaced monocle certainly argued some sort of emotional upset within himself.

In short, there was a fairly convincing case against the tutor until it came to a question of motive. There one was forced to draw on the imagination. Could his zeal for the college have carried him away to such an extent that he would wish to exterminate a morose, antisocial person like Baumann—a man who took everything he could get from Cambridge and gave nothing in return? Could he perhaps have known of Baumann's antipicated "trouble" and killed him to save possible disgrace to All Saints?

It was remotely possible; but I should not have cared to have to convince a jury.

The Case against Michael Grayling

Much as I liked Michael and although I would willingly have given him several pints of my own blood at any time that a transfusion might be required, I could not ignore the fact that there was a certain amount of superficial evidence against him.

In the first place, Baumann's death would probably solve his most urgent problem by enabling him to win the Lenox Scholarship and thus stay up and take his degree at Cambridge. But that he would resort to a deliberate murder in order to achieve this end was absolutely and utterly unthinkable.

Michael was a gentle soul, kindly and courteous to almost everyone and hard or intolerant only towards any kind of sham or pretentiousness. He abhorred cruelty and avoided it as he avoided all the less pleasant aspects of life.

And in this connection I recalled the fact that nothing had surprised me more than the cruel and postively ghoulish nature of the story which he had told me on Monday night. It had seemed so foreign to his placid, contemplative nature, so far removed from his normal philosophy. For Michael's happiness and his deeper emotions came from within. Few people suspected that his feelings went very deep. How he would act under some violent, external stimulus, even I, his closest friend, would find it difficult to say.

If he *did* kill Baumann, however, I felt sure that his reason for doing so would have been neither selfish nor personal. There would of necessity have been some factor which had not yet come to light. True, he could easily have done it as far as actual times and places were concerned.

After the lights went out he could have gained admission to Baumann's room either through the door or by the window. He would have had plenty of time to go down to his own room, find his electric flashlight, collect a tin of Brasso and some cleaning rags and do the job before I came back to my room or the lights went on again. His only difficulty would have been to avoid Somerville and Comstock on the stairs.

And then, I had noticed that Michael showed a marked aversion to discussing the crime in any of its aspects. Since Monday he had been more of a recluse than ever. For some unknown reason he had been especially anxious to avoid me. Of course he was working very hard, but there was something wrong somewhere. That much was obvious.

The Case against Camilla Lathrop

Much as I disliked to tabulate my suspicions against Michael, I felt even less inclination to raise my sharpened pencil against the girl whom I now loved more than ever. And yet—unless one believed implicity in her protestations of innocence—all of her actions on Monday were highly suspect.

In her defense, however, there was the undeniable fact that she had not been seen to leave or enter the college that night. Also she must have known that she was running the risk of instant dismissal from Newnham if she had come to "A" staircase at ten o'clock at night even on a perfectly innocent errand.

Apart from these facts in her favour there was little that could be said. She had never established any real alibi for herself. Innocent people do not faint at the word "murder" unless they are in some degree implicated; nor do nice English girls call on unknown undergraduates in their rooms unless they want to find something out pretty badly. On her own admission she knew Baumann well enough for him to give her some of his perfume. Might he not also have mentioned the place where he kept his revolver?

Again, she seemed more than anxious not to have it known that she had ever been on our staircase during Baumann's lifetime. Furthermore, she had been frank with me up to a certain point and then relapsed into complete mystery. Were these the actions of an entirely innocent person?

Perhaps, and perhaps not. Once again I should not have cared to try to convince a jury. Nevertheless, I would not have liked even so kindly a person as Horrocks to know as much as I knew about Camilla Lathrop. I was glad for her sake that it was I who was the repository of her little secrets.

The Case against Lloyd Comstock and Stuart Somerville

These two had both had the same amount of time and opportunity to kill Baumann. So far as I knew, both of them had flashlights in their rooms (kept there for use on their "push-bikes"), both of them knew where the revolver was kept and both of them were naturally quite at home on their own staircase.

With Comstock there was no visible motive for murder except a pronounced and often-proclaimed dislike. With Somerville there was the rather tenuous reason that the South African kept him out of his place on the Cambridge cricket team. Tenuous? Well, I was not so sure. Having lived for almost a year among young Englishmen, I had realized the sad truth that distinction in athletics seemed to supersede all other worldly and spiritual considerations. To be a "blood" at Cambridge meant more to the average undergraduate than the hopes of a ringside seat in heaven.

But surely Somerville, even if he remained only twelfth man on the Varsity eleven, was "bloody" enough? Perhaps—but an unathletic person like myself could be no possible judge of how much importance Stuart might attach to a cricket blue.

And yet, from the point of view of character and temperament, I would have said that Comstock was more capable than Somerville of committing a sudden act of violence. Lloyd was nervous, highly-strung and impulsive; Stuart was easy-going, good-natured and mentally lazy. Comstock would certainly have had enough intelligence to think the thing out carefully and methodically, but he would probably have ruined all at the last minute by some rash action.

If Somerville ever committed anything approaching the perfect crime, it would undoubtedly be the wildest freak of luck or accident! But, being of the "ridin', shootin' and huntin'" type of young Englishman, he should at least have known that guns and revolvers are not cleaned with Brasso!

And, although Comstock was more temperamentally fitted for murder than Somerville, I was bound to confess that he had acted far more normally since Monday than had Stuart. Once or twice I had detected a lack of frankness in Somerville's manner when we were discussing our various movements after the lights went out.

Perhaps it was only my vivid imagination, but I could not help thinking that it was to him that the inspector referred when he made his cryptic remarks about my not being the only person on the staircase who might know more than he was telling. But I also thought that there were several people to whom this remark might have applied. Almost everyone, it seemed, had something that he was anxious to hide.

The Case against Mrs. Bigger, Mrs. Fancher or Mary Smith

It was clear that these three women were in the college on Monday night and that any one of them (with the exception of Mary Smith) could have had easy access to "A" staircase if not to Baumann's actual rooms. Mrs. Bigger usually left the college at about 7 o'clock and it was presumably a mere coincidence that she should have stayed late on the fatal night.

She disliked Baumann. She knew where he kept his pistol and she probably knew where Hankin kept the keys to the outer doors or "oaks." But the idea of Mrs. Bigger's doing anything more murderous than to flick a fly with her duster was absolutely unthinkable. True, she showed an unhallowed interest in disease, death and morbid pathology, but her interest was, so it seemed, strictly objective, if not actually professional. (Was she not the worthy relict of an undertaker?)

As for Mrs. Fancher, bedder on "C" staircase, and Mary Smith, housemaid at the Master's Lodge, I knew them by sight only. Mrs. Fancher was a broad, phlegmatic woman of uncertain age. Mary was young, pretty and had what is usually described as a "wealth" of Titian red hair.

It would have cost her her job and her reputation to speak to any undergraduate, let alone go to his rooms at night. The thing was unheard of. On the rare occasions when she was obliged to cross the court, she walked hurriedly, her eyes downcast.

She was notoriously Hank's property, his inamorata, the girl with whom he was "walking out," "keeping company" or what have you. It is indeed more than possible that she lingered at the foot of "A" staircase for a word or two with her taciturn Corydon on Monday night.

Mrs. Fancher, too, doubtless paused to give valediction before escorting her two friends round to the convivial atmosphere of dog's noses at her husband's public. But there was nothing sinister in that—surely?

And yet, the Brasso? The cleaning materials? Who could have obtained them more easily than a college servant who uses such things every day in the performance of household duties? And the ignorance of firearms displayed by the choice of the cleaning materials in question? Might not the subtle analyst argue that they betrayed a female agency?

But which male of this day and generation knows exactly what implements *are* used in the care of firearms? I know I don't—or rather didn't. And I would wager that few of my intimate friends at Cambridge did either. No one, in fact, except the military-minded Horrocks or the sporting Somerville. No, the tin of Brasso, if it proved anything, merely proved that the murderer was not familiar with firearms or, at least, wished to have it believed that he was more of an amateur than he really was.

All of which amounted to precisely—nothing!

After I had dealt with Mrs. Bigger, Mrs. Fancher and Mary Smith, my imagination began to run completely amok. I worked out in elaborate detail, the case against the master, the case against any one of the Masters' guests and the case against Dr. Warren's unknown visitor who played Chopin so delicately. Then I turned whimsical and constructed an exquisite case against Hilary Fenton.

This was interesting in that it showed me the complete futility of my previous paper work. Where all the others had but slight opportunity to do this deed of darkness, I had abundant chances. Where they had but one motive, I had several. I alone could—and did—destroy the evidence of guilt. I was a foreigner, a stranger, an unknown quantity.

In short, I must (on paper) be the murderer. I was one of those dreadful people who write a mystery story in the first person and (after nineteen chapters of carefully laid false trails) calmly announce that the only point omitted was the simple fact that "I" did it all along!

My deductions, if carried to their logical conclusion would put a noose around my neck. They must be destroyed.

But, although the case against me was very strong, I am going to state quite frankly and straightforwardly that I did *not* kill Julius Baumann. I might add that, in writing this chronicle of his death, I have kept nothing back. I have faithfully recorded all the events as they happened and all my ideas as they occurred to me.

Never for one single moment have I deliberately caused the lame to stumble or the blind to go out of his way. I have kept faith with my readers by listing all suspects without personal prejudice and by working out the case against them with a calm and unbiased pencil. If I have merely succeeded in proving that I, Hilary Fenton, must have been the guilty party, then I sadly confess that my pencil was sharpened—to no point.

CHAPTER X

North by Northwest

I AM rather ashamed to admit it, but during this whole week I was happier than I had ever been in my life before. I should be an unmitigated humbug if I pretended that Baumann's death had been a matter of personal sorrow to me. True, it had been a great shock, but it had coincided with something which had proved an even greater shock to my nervous system and metabolic processes. I refer, of course, to the fact that I had fallen in love for the first time in my life.

This devastating occurrence had driven the unpleasant and gruesome aspects of the case to the background of my mind. I could enjoy the agreeable stimulation of an abstract problem. I could enjoy cutting lectures without a qualm of conscience; and my unofficial peeps behind the scenes at the stage properties of a great university made me feel pleasantly important. Then, there was the warm weather to add to my happiness. The roses were beginning to bloom in the fellows' gardens. The college lawns were unbelievably green, while the fields around Cambridge were dotted with moon-daisies, buttercups and purple vetch.

Even the old gray buildings had a jaunty, rejuvenated air; and on the undergraduates' cheeks I noticed a healthy, brownish tinge—the first promises of a deeper summer tan. And one evening, as I strolled along the banks of the Cam, I heard a nightingale, late in its wooing, expressing all the love and tragedy in life—all the emotions which I myself had been experiencing that week.

There were some signs that the much maligned English summer was actually on its way. This was part of the miracle which I was sharing with the great ghosts of Chaucer, Milton, Wordsworth and Tennyson.

For they too had lived in Cambridge; they too had (who knows?) loved their respective Camillas here, had seen the dog-roses whitening the lanes in Madingley or Grantchester and watched the fleecy clouds sail high above Great Trinity Court and King's meadow. In sharing thus their secret, the fringes of their mantle seemed to rustle constantly around me. No wonder I was happy and uplifted.

But there was one thing which slightly clouded my happiness at this period. I was worried about Michael and unhappy about our relationship which, for the past few days, had been strained and totally lacking in spontaneity. I liked Michael better than any man I had ever known.

His quiet humour, his steadiness of purpose and his English sincerity were the complement of my somewhat flamboyant flippancy and American ebullience. He seemed to possess all the characteristics which I most admired—all the qualities which were outside my own very limited reach. He had always been a real person and a real friend.

But since Monday night Michael had been unaccountably reserved, cold and unsympathetic. True, he was very busy with his work for the Lenox Scholarship. There were other competitors besides Baumann—less formidable, perhaps, but competitors none the less. I knew that he was obliged to work hard, but one is never too busy for a smile, a cheerio or a hastily snatched cigarette with a friend. But the trouble was that Michael acted almost as though he no longer regarded me as a friend.

Friday was the day of his examination. Before going off to join

Camilla at Fenners, I decided to try to catch Michael and wish him luck with his afternoon papers. I found him munching a piece of bread and marmalade over a battered copy of Homer's *Iliad.* He looked tired and despondent.

"How d'you make out this morning?" I asked with the fatuous cheerfulness one adopts with people who are going through any kind of ordeal.

He gave a noncommittal grunt.

"What is it this afternoon?"

"Greek and Latin Unseen," he replied shortly.

"Well, keep smiling, old man. Remember how Browning says that we should 'greet the unseen with a cheer.'"

"There's nothing very cheerful about it," he replied with a slow, unwilling smile.

"Bosh, Mike, don't be a chump. You know you are a snip for the schol."

Instead of laughing, as he usually did, at my exhibition of English public school colloquialism, Michael turned towards his desk and started to collect some pens and pencils. When he faced me again there was a strange expression on his countenance.

"Perhaps I am," he said slowly, "since, as you were obliging enough to tell me yourself, my chief competitor has been *eliminated.* And, some time when neither of us is quite so busy, I imagine you are going to tell me exactly how you knew the fact at least ten minutes before it—er—became a fact!"

With these words he picked up his gown and strode out of the room.

"Michael, you ass!" I called after him, but he did not stop or look around. Then, suddenly, an amazing truth began to dawn upon me. Michael must think that *I* killed Julius Baumann, or, at least, that I knew who did.

And what was more natural? I tell him that one of his competitors is going to be eliminated. Within a few moments his dead body is discovered. Why should I blame Michael for suspecting me? Had not I, on the previous night, made out a case against him—mine own familiar friend? Had I not?

But here another, even more terrible thought struck me. Might not the strange expression which I had just seen on Michael's face have been nothing more or less than—fear? What if he himself had killed Julius Baumann just before I returned to my room on Monday night?

Would not my innocent remark about elimination have been fraught with a terrifying significance—an indication that I either knew or suspected his guilt? He had heard nothing about Baumann's letter or the fact that the South African had planned to leave Cambridge. Nor could I tell him—at least, not yet. It was all a ghastly muddle.

And there were plenty of other muddles for me to think about as I walked along the narrow, winding streets of Cambridge on my way towards Fenners. But the problem which absorbed all the people I passed was the outcome of the cricket match. From stray remarks I gathered that the prognosis was none too favourable for the Varsity.

"Five wickets down for ninety," was one comment I heard. "That leaves three hundred for the last five men—and no Baumann. If only Somerville—"

But at that moment, I caught sight of a familiar figure mounted— horrors!—on a bicycle. It was Camilla Lathrop. Camilla on a "push-bike." The ways of the English female are indeed strange and past all seeking out!

I advanced towards her through the milling traffic and seized the handlebars rather in the manner of Dick Turpin.

"Please," I cried in anguish. "Please let me take this—er— vehicle. On the whole I'd rather have had the mackintosh."

She dismounted meekly and said with a seraphic smile:

"I like your cheek, Hilary Fenton."

"I'm afraid you do," I replied, rubbing it reminiscently.

After which unsentimental greeting we joined the brightly dressed throng of young men and maidens who were busily pushing their way into the playing field. I parked the offending bicycle and joined Camilla who had found a delightfully secluded spot under some elm trees.

She was wearing a light grayish-green costume which made me think (though I had never seen them) of the olive groves of Greece and the gray-eyed Pallas Athene. The cricket had just started again after the lunch interval.

As viewed from a train or any other safe distance, cricket is undoubtedly the most effective and picturesque game ever devised by men. The immaculate white flannels against the green of the English meadow—the long-legged, sturdy young giants, the grace of their seemingly casual movements—the scent of clover and the droning of bees—all these go to make up a charming picture in vivid contrast to the dusty, noisy, peanut and coca-cola atmosphere of a baseball game.

But when watched in a concentrated manner through field-glasses, or with each of its intricate points carefully explained—even when the explanations are made by the girl of the moment—cricket is, to my mind, still beautiful, perhaps, but dumb, hopelessly dumb. It lacks the virility and *élan* of baseball. It has no speed, no vigor, no vitamins. It is altogether too polite.

"Oh, well hit, Somerville," murmured Camilla, as a ball sped over the ground in our direction.

"Somerville?"

"Yes, he's batting now and he's nicely set, too. Looks like making fifty at least, if not his century."

"What on earth are they doing now? I asked presently, as the players began to move in an apparently aimless manner about the field.

"Oh, you poor American," sighed Camilla good-naturedly. "It's *over*. That means one of the bowlers has bowled six balls. Then the umpire—he's the man in the long white coat—calls *over* and another bowler starts at the other end. See, there he goes."

The bowler was taking a long run behind the wickets preparatory to hurling the ball at my handsome stairmate.

"Why doesn't he chuck the ball if he wants it to be really fast?" I asked.

"It's against the rules to bend the arm at the elbow. Well hit, sir!" Somerville had run forward and smacked the ball in a manner worthy of Babe Ruth. There was a mild burst of conservative English applause.

"But why don't they run?" I asked, pleased at my friend's success.

"Boundary," replied my mentor. "No need to run. It counts four anyhow. Six if it lands outside full pitch. Things are beginning to look up. One hundred and fifty for five wickets. Oh, damn, the captain is l. b. w."

The captain of the Varsity team, having stopped a ball on his pad, was now walking slowly towards the pavilion. Tragic voices were raised on all sides.

"But the ball didn't knock those funny little sticks down and he wasn't caught out," I exclaimed mystified. "What on earth is l. b. w.?

"Leg before wicket," sighed Camilla. "Oh, damn that umpire."

"But I distinctly saw the ball hit Somerville's pad just before in exactly the same way. Why wasn't he put out too?"

"Well, that ball either wasn't straight or it had a break on, probably. The umpire has to decide. Here's Malden. He's a stone waller. Now if only he can keep his wicket up and let Somerville do the scoring...."

I was completely bewildered. One point alone was clear to me. Great things were expected of Stuart and so far his filling of a dead man's shoes had been more than competent. He now had a chance to rescue his side. In the meantime I was happy under the elm trees—more or less alone with Camilla.

But our solitude was destined to be short-lived. A couple was approaching with purposeful strides—a large purple female in spectacles with an etiolated male bringing up the rear. A well known voice started to quack:

"Why, Millie, here you are again. Put your mac down here, Perce."

I winced at the abbreviation of Camilla's name, but she hid any annoyance she may have felt with admirable fortitude.

"Why, Dorothy, how nice!" She jumped up to make a place beside her, then added with a mischievous smile, "By the way, let me introduce Mr. Hilary Fenton."

"Ah, Mr. Fenton and I are old pals, but I didn't know that you two were." Dorothy Dupuis looked at us for a moment with myopic suspicion.

"I do think Somerville is a *nib!*" she breathed, gazing rapturously towards the cricket pitch. "A real nib! He's going to save the match. And he's in your coll., isn't he, Mr. Fenton?"

"Yes, and he's on my staircase."

"Well, you must give me an intro. some time," she said archly. "Now don't be jel., darling." She turned towards her fiancé who was fingering a pimple on his chin and gazing abstractedly at the scoring board.

"He's made his fifty," muttered the prelate presumptive. "That's two hundred for six wickets and Malden is blocking like Ely Cathedral. There's one chance in a thousand—"

For awhile I let the cricket take care of itself and gradually dropped off into a pleasant state of day-dreaming. Suddenly there began to creep over me that uneasy sensation that someone was staring at me. A man standing a few yards away seemed vaguely familiar. Could it be—? Yes, it was—Inspector Horrocks.

Now, what on earth was he doing at a cricket match when he was supposed to be occupied on two important cases? And why was he scrutinizing Camilla and me so persistently? Fully awake, I jumped up and went over to him.

"Hello, Inspector," I said, approaching from the rear. "So you are not too busy to enjoy the sport of men?"

Horrocks put one colossal forefinger up to his nose and murmured with a cryptic smile, "Baumann wasn't the only person in this business who liked cricket, Mr. Fenton."

"Hot on the trail, are you?" I asked with interest, "or just playing hookey?"

"I don't care for hookey, Mr. Fenton. Oh, well hit, sir," he cried with admiration, as a ball from Somerville's bat soared over our heads for a boundary (six runs—*vive* Camilla!) "Your friend will make his century today or I'm a Dutchman. He's up to eighty-six now. It's a great chance for him, Mr. Fenton, a great chance."

But whether or not there was a sinister inflection in his voice I did not have time to consider, for at this moment a pleasant-looking man came up to him, touched his elbow and passed him an orange envelope. Horrocks opened the telegram and read it through slowly. As he did so, his florid face almost rivaled the purple of Dorothy Dupuis' dress. The two men conferred in whispers. At length the inspector turned towards me and handed me the telegram.

"You might as well read this, Mr. Fenton, seeing as how we are old friends and have no secrets from each other, like you might say, sir."

It came from a town called Oakham (Rutland) and it stated that the authorities there were holding a man who answered to the broadcasted description of William North.

"Matter of fifty or sixty miles," I heard the pleasant-looking man say. "The car's waiting outside."

"Can't I come, too?" I cried. "Rutland is the smallest county in England, isn't it? So Oakham must be the smallest county town."

Horrocks smiled broadly. "Plenty of room for a friend," he said casually.

"Oh, but—" for the first time since Monday I had forgotten Camilla's existence. As I looked towards her, I saw that she was surrounded by a noisy group of undergraduates. "Just let me park my obligations," I murmured.

I went over to the little cluster of boys and girls beneath the elms and whispered an explanation to Camilla. At the word "North" she seemed to start and the colour rushed to her cheeks.

"Yes, Hilary, go—please go," she cried eagerly. "And be nice to him, poor man, and make them be nice to him, too. Remember that—"

"—there but for the grace of God goes Hilary Fenton," I finished, kissing my fingertips.

But she paid no attention to me for her head was turned away as if to hide tears of pity.

I rejoined the two men and we all three piled into the front seat of the waiting Morris. Johnson, the pleasant-looking man, was a good driver and we were soon making fast time along the Huntington road.

"What direction are we going?" I asked.

"North by northwest," replied Johnson. "We hit the Great North Road very soon."

"Very suitable," I murmured.

We passed through Huntington, famous as the birthplace of Oliver Cromwell, and continued towards Stilton, even more famous as the birthplace of the eponymous cheese. Here a signpost bearing the word "Peterborough" caught my eye.

"Are we going through Peterborough?" I asked excitedly. "I'd give my back teeth to see that Cathedral."

Horrocks cocked an eye good-humoredly at Johnson.

"It's not really out of our way," said the driver smiling, "and Bill North is a good sort. He wouldn't mind waiting."

"I'll give you exactly five minutes," said the inspector as we drew up outside the cathedral close. He produced an enormous watch from his pocket and smiled in a paternal manner.

Five minutes to see one of England's grandest cathedrals! And me without a Baedeker! Another American tragedy.

I did have time, however, to admire the clerestory and triforium and to crick my neck in looking up at the perfect Norman woodwork of the ceiling. I stood for a few seconds by the tomb of Henry VIII's first and most unfortunate wife. Then I came out and bought a picture postcard to send to my father.

We jumped in the car and continued on our interrupted journey through the fast-receding fenland. Some deep, primeval instinct made me love this flat unpromising landscape even better than the more prtentiously picturesque sections of England. Was not my own name Fenton—undoubtedly a corruption of Fentown—and was it not possible that in this very neighbourhood my ancestors first saw the light of day and had their peaceful beings?

After leaving the fen district behind us, we passed through Stamford, the Oxford of the Middle Ages, with its magnificent churches, almshouses and its atmosphere of ancient learning and intellectual aspiration. Within twenty minutes we were entering Oakham and all other considerations went out of my mind at the prospect of seeing one of the most famous figures in English criminal history.

The car finally drew up in front of the small brick police station and we all entered the building together. A bobby took us into a back room where a slight, bearded man sat quietly reading an old, musty volume.

He looked up as we entered and I noticed that he had a broad, intellectual forehead, thinning gray hair and sad eyes whose expression seemed vaguely familiar. A smile spread over his face as Johnson advanced, holding out his hand.

So this was the famous William North whose moment of madness had set England talking for twenty years. This quiet, scholarly figure was the desperate criminal lunatic whose face had, for the past week been on the front page of every newspaper in the country. And I had expected him to look like a cross between Charlie Peace and Tarzan of the Apes! It was unbelievable.

"Why, Bill," Johnson was saying, "here you are at last. We've been missing you up at the home. You shouldn't have gone off that way." His tone was that of an indulgent mother whose child has been caught in the larder.

William North smiled again—a sad, dreamy smile. "I'm sorry if I've inconvenienced you," he said gently, "but I'm quite ready to come back now. I had to get into a decent library somehow or other. I had to get hold of this book."

Johnson scratched his head in good-humoured bewilderment. "What's that?" he asked.

"Ravisius Textor's *Officina*. I had a theory that Rabelais used it to compile his famous lists. I believe I'm right."

"Well, you can bring it along with you—and we've had the piano tuned while you were away," said the warden cheerfully. "The superintendent is looking forward to hearing some more Chopin."

But I could stand no more. The kindness, the incredible kindness of these two officials moved me more than any display of coarseness or brutality would have done. Truly England is a wonderful country for concealing the iron hand beneath the suède glove of gentleness. No wonder it has a lower criminal record than any other country!

I strolled about Oakham in the twilight and gazed idly at the old butter market and stocks—grim relics of the days when police authorities were not so kind as Inspector Horrocks—its fine old church and school where I could hear the happy laughter of the boys as they came out of "prep." It was a charming, peaceful town.

When I returned to the police station, the formalities had apparently been concluded and North was sitting in the front seat of the car next to Johnson. I was introduced as a young American who had come because he wanted to see Peterborough Cathedral.

"A beautiful place," commented North with a reminiscent light in his eyes, "but it's a pity that they moved the body of Mary, Queen of Scots." Involuntarily he spoke of this event (which occurred in the reign of James I) as though it had happened last week. His mind, apparently, no longer belonged in this century. The present did not exist for him. He showed no disinclination whatsoever to being taken back to the "home."

"You're very fond of Chopin, aren't you, Mr. North?" I asked suddenly.

"Why, yes," he replied with his sad, faraway smile, "Chopin is the only composer whose works I care to play now. There is another world quality about his music which seems to be especially written for those who are—er—barred from this world and all its activities." He turned towards Johnson. "I'm glad you had the piano tuned," he said simply.

We reached the outskirts of Cambridge at about half past eleven. After bidding my companions good night, I beckoned Horrocks aside and whispered into his ear.

"Did you notice that suit which North is wearing? No? Well, examine the buttonholes and you will see something interesting. The person to whom it originally belonged was obviously in the habit of wearing a monocle."

Horrocks solemnly placed one forefinger along the side of his nose and closed one eye. "It doesn't always pay to see everything, Mr. Fenton. Good night, sir."

Apparently I was not the only person who had guessed the identity of Dr. Warren's visitor on Monday night.

I strolled leisurely towards All Saints, thinking about the extraordinary events of this extraordinary day. Everything had been so contradictory. Everybody had insisted upon acting in the way that one would least expect. The staid Dr. Warren had entertained in his rooms a desperate, hunted criminal.

The criminal had turned out to be a scholar and a gentleman who played Chopin and talked like the Dons at high table. His relentless hunters had behaved like angels of peace and mercy instead of hard-boiled sleuths. They had even halted their chase to allow a young American dilettante to look at a cathedral. And the other dramatis personae were no less topsy turvy.

Camilla, the mysterious midnight vision of my dreams, was a nice flesh and blood girl who liked to watch cricket matches and rode a bicycle. There was nothing sinister about Dorothy Dupuis except her abbreviations. The invariable Michael was sulking like a schoolboy while Somerville—

"Hello, Fenton on Torts." I heard my name called from across the street. "Come on, chaps, lets de-bag Hilarious Hilary from Phila., Pa., the son of Fenton on Legal Theory ... the son and only heir ... oh, come let us de-bag him!"

Four youths were advancing towards me. It was obvious from their gait that they had been entertaining themselves well, but not too wisely. I stood my ground.

"What was the result of the cricket match?" I asked nervously, feeling that something was expected of me.

Stuart groaned. "Listen, you chaps, he doesn't even know that we licked the M. C. C. He doesn't even know that his own blue-eyed boy friend made one hundred and sixty-eight, not out. If that isn't a case for de-bagging ..."

"De-bag him ... de-bag him!" cried the others.

I shall never know whether or not they really intended to commit violence on my nether garments, for at this moment some one called out:

"Look out, chaps! The Progs."

There was a general scurrying in all directions as the proctor turned the corner, followed by his two attendant bulldogs in their top hats and black coats. These are the University police and all gownless or inebriated undergraduates flee before them like leaves before the winds of winter.

Above the white band round the proctor's neck I saw the stern, pale face of Dr. Warren. Beneath the old-fashioned top hat of the younger of the two bulldogs I caught a glimpse of Thomas Hankin. They advanced towards us in perfect phalanx. Somerville was seized.

"The proctor would like to speak to you, please, sir," said the deferential voice of our staircase gyp.

"Damn your eyes, Hank!"

But I waited to hear no more for the other "buller" was moving menacingly towards me. I fled to the sanctuary of my college. Once within its precincts I knew that I was safe.

As I entered the gates, I noticed that the hands of the clock pointed to five minutes before midnight. A few moments later and my escapade would have cost me thirteen and four pence. As it was, I had come in without my cap and gown, which would set me back to the tune of six and eight pence.

Well, the day had been worth it!

CHAPTER XI

Murder in the Court

SATURDAY morning at Cambridge is a moment of respite. It is the death of each week's life, intended by God and undergraduate as a period for sleep and for forgetting. And after my hectic Friday I had hoped to slumber on until it was time for that hybrid meal technically known as "brunch"—a movable feast midway between breakfast and lunch. But Fate had decreed otherwise; for, at the premature hour of 7:30am, I was brought back to life and all its grim realities with a very decided jerk.

"Hilary, Hilary, wake up, man!"

Someone was tugging at my bedclothes and shaking me none too gently by the shoulders. Through one half-opened eye I took in a hazy impression of Lloyd Comstock in pyjamas and dressing-gown with his dark hair sticking out in all directions. He looked like a disgruntled golliwog.

"Listen, man, you must listen," he urged. "If I don't have someone to talk to I shall go stark, staring mad. I've just had the most horrible experience...."

I turned toward the wall. "Let me dream again," I murmured, pulling the covers over my ears. "It's too early for horrors."

"But, my God, man. I've just—I've just discovered a dead body—a corpse. Here in the college." His voice was shrill with excitement.

I sat up, not quite certain whether I was asleep or awake.

"What?" I asked, bewildered.

"About an hour ago, in the court. The police are there now. They told me not to talk, but everyone must have seen it by this time. When I came away, there was a crowd of servants and four policemen, and oh, it was too utterly—beastly."

He paused and looked around, wildly. I jumped out of bed, ran to my cupboard and poured a stiff tot of brandy.

"Here, take this," I said, half choking him in my efforts to get it down his throat, "and that is what comes of getting up at such ungodly hours as you do!"

But he did not smile. The neat brandy had made him blink and splutter. Presently he gasped out:

"I got up about six. It was such a ripping morning for a stroll. I just couldn't stay in bed. Besides—" he added, running a hand through his hair, "I've been sleeping rottenly since—since Monday."

"Yes, but—"

"Well, I was going across the court to the baths when I suddenly noticed a top hat lying on the ground under the white lilac bush just by the front door of the Master's Lodge. You know?"

I nodded.

He gulped again.

"Well, I thought some of the fellows had probably been having a rag last night—celebrating the cricket match or something—so I stopped to pick it up. As I did so, I saw a man's boot sticking out from under the bush.

"Of course, I thought it must be some sort of dummy—a wax figure that some bright boy had pinched from a tailor's shop. I went up closer to have a look and—and then I saw that it wasn't part of a rag at all—that it was grim earnest—"

He paused for a moment and then continued more slowly:

"It was Hank lying there—our Hank, all covered with blood and dressed up in his black clothes like an—undertaker. He was stone dead and there was a silly smile on his face, you know, the sort you see on the effigies of Guy Fawkes."

His teeth were chattering so I threw something 'round his shoulders and poured some more brandy. "Buck up, Lloyd," I exhorted him, though I felt anything but bucked up myself.

"Well, I've no idea what I did next. I imagine I must have called the porter because all at once there seemed to be a crowd of people round me. Dr. Warren was there and he looked so funny with his monocle on top of green striped pyjamas—and the Dean had put on his surplice obviously in mistake for his dressing gown. Oh, it was bloody, bloody funny."

Comstock was dangerously near the point of hysteria. I looked at him helplessly. Presently he continued in a slightly more normal tone:

"And then the inspector came—what's his name—Horrocks. I heard Dr. Warren say that Hank must have died shortly after midnight. And that he had been stabbed in four places. There was some talk about a knife. Then the policemen began to turn everyone away. They told me to wait in my room until I was sent for. And now—"

"And now you are going to have some good strong coffee," I said with decision. "My God, poor old Hankin! You just lie down, Lloyd, while I get some breakfast. You look all in, man."

I tumbled into some clothes and made a brew of coffee. Comstock's hand trembled as he took the cup but he appeared eager to discuss the matter. In fact, his state of mind improved visibly as he unburdened himself. We talked for about an hour and then a policeman appeared and told us laconically that we were both wanted. We followed him down to Dr. Warren's rooms where an animated scene was in progress.

Half-wrapped in a white napkin, on the table lay a small knife of primitive design. It seemed to be the centrepiece of the room and focussed everyone's attention. The senior tutor was standing near the bay window, staring at it gloomily through his monocle. Horrocks was seated at the table, and was in the act of dismissing Mrs. Bigger, who stood, poised for flight, near the door as we entered.

"Well, sir," she was crying with the righteous indignation of one who suspects that her word has been doubted, "if it's the last thing I say when they come to screw me down in me corfin, I shall sit up and tell them that that there knife belonged to Mr. Baumann, that I shall. And it 'ung above 'is mantel and cluttered up my cleaning every morning until Monday last—and as soon as I kleps me eyes on it, I sez ..."

"All right, Mrs. Bigger. Thank you." Horrocks' voice cut through her monologue.

The bedmaker stalked majestically from the room. Then the inspector turned toward me and pointed at the knife on the table. "Now, Mr. Fenton, have you ever seen this knife before?"

I replied that to the best of my knowledge and belief, it had been the property of my South African neighbour; that it had been in his room last Monday morning but I had not seen it since. No, I could not be positive that it had not been there on Monday night when I discovered the body.

I recognized it by the primitive design on the handle. I knew it was a Kaffir knife—probably one of the crude weapons used by the African savages. Baumann had had a number of similar native trophies in his room. Dr. Warren nodded as if to signify that he agreed with me.

Horrocks then asked Lloyd Comstock to go through the details of his finding Hankin's body. My stairmate had now completely recovered his composure and went through the recital in a calm, even voice. He added nothing to what he had told me earlier that morning.

The college porter was next sent for and questioned. He told the inspector that Hankin had come in from his duties as bulldog at about five minutes past twelve on the previous night. He had then gone straight over to the Master's Lodge in the hopes (so he said) of catching a glimpse of his girl. Dr. Warren had come in shortly afterwards.

Hank slept in a little room just above the porter's lodge and next to that occupied by the porter himself. He had never heard him come back to his room, but he had paid no attention to this fact since Hankin, who was anything but talkative, often went straight upstairs without speaking or even saying good night.

The porter expressed himself as quite certain he had seen no strangers or suspicious looking characters hanging about the court. He would have sent them about their business at once. No one had come in after Dr. Warren with the exception of Mr. Somerville, who had rung the bell at 12:16am according to the records.

The young gentleman, he added, had a paper cap on his head and seemed to be in a slightly tipsy condition; he was not wearing academic dress and—here the porter coughed slightly and cleared his throat—he had appeared to be amused by the fact that he had just been "progged" and by his own gyp at that!

"That is quite correct," said the tutor. "Hankin was one of my bulldogs last night. We caught Somerville shortly before midnight without a gown."

At this point Horrocks recalled one of the policemen, who left the room and returned in a few minutes. He was followed by Mary Smith, the housemaid at the Master's lodge.

She was dressed in a black alpaca dress and the spotless white apron which makes English domestic servants so picturesque. A small cotton cap was perched on the top of her magnificent red hair. The poor girl was snivelling into a handkerchief as she entered, and her usually pretty face was swollen and distorted with grief.

The inspector rose from his chair as though she had been a duchess and patted her into a seat. For a few moments she cried noiselessly without speaking. At length she looked up and made a helpless little gesture which seemed to signify that she was ready to answer any questions.

"Your name?" asked the inspector gently.

"Mary Smith, sir," she replied into her handkerchief.

"And you live—"

"At Trumpington, sir, alone with my mother—that is when I'm not at the lodge, sir."

"Yes, yes. You were engaged to marry Thomas Hankin, I believe?"

"Oh, yes, sir." Here she looked across at Dr. Warren. "And I didn't mean no 'arm meeting him like that outside the lodge door, sir. I know as 'ow I didn't ought to of, not reely, sir, but Tom he worked so 'ard and it wasn't often we had a chance to see each other. He was saving up his money, sir, to buy us a 'ome in South Africa and—oh, oh—" She burst into tears.

Horrocks looked at her sympathetically. "And you were the last person to see him alive?" he asked softly.

The girl looked at him sharply and her tears seemed to dry up as if by magic.

"Oh, no, sir," she said almost eagerly. "The gentleman who spoke to Hankin when we were by the front door. He was the last, sir."

Everyone was staring at Mary Smith with interest. There was a long pause.

"Suppose you tell us exactly what happened," said the inspector. "In your own words."

With another apprehensive glance in the direction of Dr. Warren, the maid replied in a low voice: "Well, sir, I knew as 'ow Tom—that's Hankin, sir—would be finished bull-dogging soon after twelve, so I waited for him by the front door of the lodge. The master and the mistress had gone to bed long since. I didn't see no 'arm and there wasn't any of the young gentlemen about."

"No, no, quite natural," said Horrocks hurriedly. "Don't distress yourself."

"Well, Hankin came at about ten minutes past twelve and we—er—talked a minute or two, sir, and then I heard footsteps coming—a man's footsteps. I went back inside the front door cos I didn't want no one to see me there, sir, and I closed it a tiny crack and waited a minute.

"And then I heard Tom say, 'Certainly, sir, I'll come at once,' and when I opened the door the two of them had moved off together and that—that was the last I seen of him, sir, the very last. No good night, no good-bye, sir." The handkerchief was again produced.

"Did you recognize the voice of this individual who spoke to Hankin?" interposed Dr. Warren.

The maid looked at him timidly. "No, sir," she said, dabbing at her eyes.

"Would you say, from the manner in which Hankin replied, that it was one of the tutors who spoke to him or one of the gentlemen?" asked Horrocks with unconscious humor.

The ghost of a smile flitted for a moment around Dr. Warren's grim mouth.

"I didn't catch what he said, sir, but Hankin answered very respectful like. But then, he was always respectful even to the young gentlemen, sir."

"I see. But it wasn't a fellow servant?" The girl shook her head. Horrocks turned to Dr. Warren. "Have you any idea who it could have been, Colonel?" he asked deferentially.

"I have nothing to add to the evidence I have already given," replied the tutor coldly.

"You two young gentlemen have no idea?" He turned towards Comstock and me. We both shook our heads. There was another long moment of silence.

"I hate to say such a thing," suddenly interjected Dr. Warren, "but I should say that it was probably Hankin's murderer." (There was a gasp from Mary Smith.) "When all's said and done, he must have died between twelve and twelve-thirty. It is a great pity that this young woman cannot have been more precise. Was the man tall or short, for example? Did he wear a gown? Was his voice loud or soft?" He looked at the housemaid quizzically through his monocle.

"I didn't see him, sir, and I couldn't hear what he said," she answered humbly. "There was only a crack of the door open and Hankin was standing in front of him. But if I'd only known," she added with some spirit, "as how it might have been his murderer, sir ..."

"Yes, yes," interrupted Horrocks, who appeared anxious to avoid anything in the nature of an emotional outburst. "And now, I wonder if you could tell us whether Hankin had any enemies, whether there was anyone who might have had a grudge against him?"

The girl raised her head and, for the first time, I noticed what good, intelligent eyes she had. In the general way one had only a vague impression of a pretty face topped by abundant auburn hair; but now it was obvious to me that she was no fool.

"Enemies? Oh, no, sir. Hankin didn't have no enemies, least not as I knew of. He always worked very hard and was the saving, quiet sort, sir. He didn't have no time to make friends or enemies."

"Did he ever mention Mr. Baumann to you—the young gentleman who died last Monday night?"

"No, sir, not particular. I think he did say once as how he come from South Africa, too, and how he was homesick like."

"He never hinted that he knew anything about Mr. Baumann's—er—accident, I suppose? Or anything about Mr. Baumann's past life that might account for his death?"

"No, sir."

The inspector looked at her fixedly for a moment and then said very slowly and distinctly: "But several people have told me that Hankin had been rather strange and—er—different since Monday night. He seemed to have something on his mind—to be worried. Now, you were closer to him than anyone else. Did you notice anything of the sort?"

The girl looked nervously towards Dr. Warren. His presence seemed to fascinate and frighten her at the same time. The tutor, evidently feeling that he was the cause of her embarrassment, rose and went into another room. A look of relief passed over Mary's face.

"Well, since you mention it, sir," she stammered, "Hankin had been sort of, well, different since last Monday. Once or twice he seemed like he was going to tell me something and then—he was not one to talk much, sir. But only last night, just before that man came up and spoke to him, he was saying as how there'd been funny things going on on 'A' staircase and funny visitors coming and going—"

(Was it my guilty conscience, or had she turned her eyes deliberately towards me?)

"Was that all?"

"Yes, sir, and then the man came up and spoke to him and I closed the door."

"So you think that perhaps Hankin knew something about Mr. Baumann's death—something that he hadn't told?"

The maid rose from her chair with simple dignity. "I only know what I have already told you, sir."

It was obvious to the inspector and, indeed, to all of us, that nothing further could be gained by additional cross-questioning. The thing was too recent, everyone was too much upset by the tragedy to be able to give testimony that was either valuable or constructive. We all needed time to elapse before we could get a proper sense of perspective.

The hearing was adjourned and I strolled out into the court with Lloyd Comstock. The college looked more like a Hollywood attempt to represent Cambridge than an actual corner of the great university itself.

A motion picture cameraman was busily photographing various corners of the old building and a group of undergraduates were making theatrical gestures to each other in animated conversation. Newspaper reporters were buttonholing recalcitrant policemen, whilst college servants stood around with empty trays like so many errand boys.

The whole thing gave the impression of a badly arranged set in an indifferently produced amateur performance. The shock seemed temporarily to have upset even the immemorial dignity of Cambridge.

While Comstock and I stood by the foot of our staircase, Michael came down with a book under his arm.

"You've heard about it?" I asked.

He nodded, looking with disgust at the garish crowd at the far end of the court. "Can't they clear up that mess?" he murmured. "It's a disgrace." And without another word he strode off through the main gateway.

No sooner had he disappeared than Stuart Somerville's door opened and the blond young cricketer emerged. He was wearing a bathrobe and his hair was dishevelled. I noticed that his usually candid eyes were slightly bloodshot and his cheeks were pale beneath their light coat of tan. The roses and raptures of a heroic yesterday had been replaced by the lilies and languors of this tragic morning.

"Tough luck on Hank," he said, anticipating our question. "He was a good egg, too, even if he did prog me last night. Mrs. Bigger has just been expounding on his virtues though I must confess that she has discovered them rather late in the day. Cripes, but my head is splitting! I need a cold tub."

He moved off towards the bathrooms and Comstock, who was still in his dressing gown, started to follow him. For a moment I stood alone, engrossed with my own thoughts.

"Well, Mr. Fenton," said a voice at my elbow, "there are certain aspects of this case which will no doubt be a source of great personal satisfaction to you."

I wheeled round to find myself looking into Horrocks' paternal countenance.

"How come?" I asked, puzzled.

"Well, sir, if Hankin was killed after midnight, that certainly eliminates some people who couldn't possibly have been in the college at that time, like as you might say sir. And if they weren't guilty in this case, they probably didn't have anything to do with Baumann's death either. My guess is that one person was responsible for both."

"It certainly lets poor old North out," I said guardedly. "If ever anyone had a cast iron alibi for his movements last night—a police inspector, a keeper and an irreproachable undergraduate."

"Come, come, Mr. Fenton," he smiled genially, "you know I wasn't referring to Bill North."

With this cryptic utterance he left me and started to disperse the newspaper and cameramen who clustered round the Master's lodge like vultures hovering over a piece of carrion.

It was a few moments before the full implication of his remarks began to dawn upon me. Now how the deuce did the old fox know that I had just been feeling relieved that Camilla was now cleared at last? For at 12:30 last night she was undoubtedly safe in her bed at Newnham.

And if he knew that I was relieved, he must have guessed that I had been worried about her previously. Well, the only explanation was that Herbert Horrocks had missed his vocation; he ought to have been on the halls in a thought-reading act. Sometimes the man was decidedly uncanny.

CHAPTER XII

Varsity Rag

CAMBRIDGE, apparently is proof against all outward chances and inward circumstances. It goes serenely on. Dynasties may totter, currencies may crash and a sick world may writhe in postwar agonies. But undergraduates still attend or cut their lectures. They plan ther rags, they hold their debates at the Union and they continue to exchange rather painful persiflage on religion, sex and communism over pale tea and improbable cakes from Matthews. So it has been, so it shall always be.

Yet I do not mean to imply for one moment that Cambridge is heartless or indifferent. On the contrary, it is as awake and aware as any place in the world. Having been in existence since the 13th century, it has seen cataclysms, wars, heresies, revolutions and schisms. Long years of wisdom and experience have taught it to realize the ephemeral nature of things temporal.

Even a sensational murder within its gates, therefore, could not be expected to clog the wheels of its eternal machinery. One unfortunate college servant had been killed in a small corner of one of its smaller colleges. Hankin undoubtedly was dead; but some 7,000 members of the university were still living. Life—and Cambridge—must go on.

But it did come as rather a surprise to me when, after leaving the somewhat vitiated atmosphere of All Saints Court, I went out into Kings Parade and found that a rag was in progress. Saturday morning at noon is the classical time for Cambridge rags, and this one now seemed like the return to normal after a crisis or comic relief following a period of tragedy.

And it was one of the most amusing and elaborate rags I had ever seen. Apparently it had originated out of a recent debate at the Union. The subject of this debate had been—*That this house deplores the growing influence of women in the activities and management of the University.* The motion had, surprisingly for Cambridge, been lost. The house obviously was far from deploring the growing influence, etc. Something had to be done about it. Hence this rag.

The streets were lined with undergraduates who stood with bowed heads in postures of mock mourning, as a hearse was pulled slowly by. The coffin bore the inscription in large black letters *the last Cambridge male*. Following the hearse was a group of plain, intellectual students, dressed in severe feminine garments with spectacles on the tips of their noses and dizzy women's hats perched on their heads. They bore a banner with the legend *Cambridge dons of the future.*

Close on their heels was a carefully picked party of pretty youths dressed in the most alluring feminine garments. Each one carried a heavy chain to which was attached a large, hairy-chested football hero, clad in the sackcloth and ashes of desperation and slavery.

Now and again these wretched victims would raise a tattered standard on which *votes for men* had been scribbled and then defaced by daubs of mud and stains suggestive of rotten eggs. Each movement towards insubordination produced a twitch of the chain from the dainty undergraduette at the other end of it. To an American like myself the whole allegory seemed almost too true to be funny.

The traffic of Cambridge was obliged to come to a complete standstill or go by another street. Proctors and bulldogs rushed madly about in a kind of impotent frenzy. The policemen, however, looked on with a kind of blasé resignation, though one unfortunate young "Robert" was foolish enough to try to make way through the crush for a passing Rolls Royce. He was promptly deprived of his helmet and sat on by a number of stalwart undergraduates.

The feminists swept all before them. And, as I looked at those young men dressed as women, a sudden inspiration struck me. How clean-cut, how clear their profiles were. Might it not have been some such vision which I saw last Monday on the darkened stairway, the night when Julius Baumann was murdered?

How easy for a nice looking young man to put on the clothes of a woman, drench himself in perfume and thus baffle a chance observer as to his sex. Any one of the boys dressed as girls for this rag—boys who were well-known for their histrionic achievements in the Footlights and C. U. A. D. S.—could have walked down Piccadilly in female attire without attracting undue attention. Supposing one or the other of them had had a spite against Baumann?

This led me to think of the undergraduates in All Saints who might conceivably have passed as women. There were plenty of them. Even the people on "A" staircase were not beyond suspicion on this score. Lloyd Comstock was small, dark, with regular features and unobtrusive extremities. He played female parts occasionally at the Footlights.

Somerville could have been made up to look like a remarkably handsome Amazon, and even Michael, though he was what was technically known as broad in the beam, might have passed muster in an age where the sexes are almost indistinguishable anyhow. The whole thing had given me furiously to think.

The procession had now paused outside the gates of Corpus. The horses that drew the hearse had seated themselves in the middle of the road and were mopping their sweaty faces. The "last male" was sitting up in his coffin and eating a doughnut.

The female dons were regaling themselves with large tankards of beer, while the beautiful undergraduates had produced enormous pipes at which they puffed uncomfortably but ostentatiously. The muscular athletes, still in chains, were producing knitting from their reticules and talked to one another in mincing voices.

The proctors were still running up and down, scribbling names and colleges on their pads, and trying to combine an air of insouciance with the I-was-young-myself-once expression which usually means that someone is going to get sent down the next day.

Finally hunger, more potent than police or proctors, dispersed the crowd and the undergraduates betook themselves lunchward. The rag was over but it had left me with the germ of an idea.

After I had made up for my scanty breakfast by a substantial lunch in Hall, I found myself strolling idly about near the college notice boards with a crowd of other undergraduates. The words, "Lenox Scholarship" caught my ear and I pushed myself forward to see the announcement 'round which people were clustering. The results of the examination had been posted. A brief glance showed me that Michael Donwell Grayling was the successful candidate.

With one whoop of delight I rushed over to "A" staircase, barely stopping to pick up a typewritten, unstamped envelope which lay on the bottom step addressed to me. Michael was in his room. Inhibitions, petty misunderstandings and all other complications were thrown to the winds. I ran up to my friend and almost embraced him in my enthusiasm.

"Michael, you old horse thief," I shouted. "Thank the Lord something decent has happened at last and now you won't have to leave Cambridge to teach smelly little boys. Oh, you egg, you bright-eyed boy ... I'm tickled pink, I'm tickled skinny."

Michael looked at me soberly. There was a smile on his face but his eyes were still tired. "Thanks awfully, Hilary, old man. It's ripping of you to be so pleased. I'm bucked about it myself, too, of course. But—"

"But nothing. The thing is over and done with. You've won it and there are no buts."

"There is always the thought of a dead man's shoes and the knowledge that I could never have got it but for a terrible accident."

"Accident my foot," I said tactlessly.

"Exactly," he replied quietly. And then we both looked at each other awkwardly and did not speak, though each knew what the other was thinking.

Whether or not an explanation might have been immediately forthcoming, I cannot say, for at this moment the door was thrown open and Lloyd Comstock and Stuart Somerville burst in.

"Hail to Grayling," cried Stuart, who appeared to have recovered from his hangover. "All hail to Grayling who has brought honor to a much dishonored staircase. May his children be many and may his daughters be as the polished corners of the temple."

"Oh, shut up," said Michael, blushing furiously as Comstock shook him by the hand. "Polished daughters, indeed! Can't you wish me anything better than that, Somerville?"

"All right, then," cried the irrepressible Stuart. "They shall make you a fellow of the college and you shall write dull text-books like Popper Fenton, Senior on Torts. I can see those endless marginal notes—*emendavit amplissime Grayling*.

"And each year you'll get grimmer and grimmer like the Merry Monocle, and finally you will discover that Livy didn't write Livy or that Ovid never had a love affair in his life. You will be famous and then, when you are old and full of years like the Master—"

"That reminds me," interrupted Comstock, "the Old Pill has invited me to tea tomorrow."

The nickname, by which the undergraduates of All Saints referred to their venerable Master, Dr. Martineau Hyssop, was not as derogatory as it may sound to American ears. The word "pill" is less a term of reproach in England than it is in the States. In this instance it was merely a play on the purgative nature of the Master's last name.

"I've been asked, too," said Michael, "But I've been wondering whether, in view of Hank's death and all the consequent fuss, he will expect us to go."

I tore open the envelope which was in my hand. It was an engraved card announcing the fact that the Master of All Saints requested the pleasure of Mr. Fenton's company to tea on Sunday, the following day.

Stuart had walked over to the door, thrown it open and was examining the landing outside with mock seriousness.

"What on earth are you doing, Somerville?" I asked.

"Just trying to see if I couldn't pry the staircase loose from its moorings and take it along with us tomorrow. Apparently he wants the whole show, woodwork, banisters and all. His invitation is wholesale. Even I have been asked, and he actually got my name right!"

Somerville had never forgiven the Master for invariably mixing him up with some obscure and pimply freshman. Another grievance was that, having once seen him in the court, talking to the captain of the college boats, Dr. Hyssop had said kindly, "Well, well, are you two gentlemen up for Littlego?" The mistake had obviously rankled.

"Well, I think we ought to call up his secretary and ask if we are really wanted," said Comstock. "The Old Pill is a pal of your dad's, Hilary. Why don't you do it?"

"All right," I answered. "I'm going up the river this afternoon and I'll do it on my way out. Coming along with me, Mike?"

Michael nodded.

"Okay. I'll call for you in about ten minutes."

I went up to my room where Mrs. Bigger was wearily cleaning up the remains of my breakfast things.

"Oh, me 'ead, me pore 'ead," she complained. "There's 'eads in my family, Mr. Fenton. We run to 'eads, so to speak, and mine is splitting like it was caught in a nutcracker."

"Well, why not sit down and rest a few minutes and take off that heavy hat," I suggested mildly.

She started and looked at me as though I had made an improper suggestion, as indeed I unwittingly had.

"Mr. Fenton," she said solemnly, "seeing as 'ow you are a Hamerican you couldn't be expected to know that there is a statue—a university statue—which says that no bedmaker shall remove 'er 'at in the presence of the young gentlemen. Why, sir, it would cost me my position if I was so much as to take out one of me 'atpins." The perennial ostrich plumes quivered in asseveration.

The idea that the sight of Mrs. Bigger's braided tresses might be a snare and a temptation to the hot-blooded undergraduate was too much for my gravity. I laughed weakly as Mrs. Bigger subsided onto my sofa. And indeed she looked completely worn out, poor soul.

Without a word I poured out some of the brandy I had used that morning for Comstock and handed her the glass. Before taking it, she looked furtively around her as though she expected Hank's admonitory ghost to pop out of the gyp cupboard and summon her to renewed activity.

"Sich goings on," she said, sipping appreciatively at my Hennessy. "Sich going and carryings on I never did see, not in my long years of bedmaking. But I knew as 'ow it was coming, Mr. Fenton. All last week I had a feeling in me bones that something was going to turn out wrong.

"Three times I dreamed of me great uncle Alfred, 'im as was took with the tapeworms and ate six full meals a day without puttin' any more flesh on 'is bones than there is on a clothes prop.

"'Louisa,' 'e sez, 'I sees a dark cloud 'anging over you, Louisa. Trouble, trouble and no rest for them weary feet of yours!' And now what with all Mr. 'Ankin's work for me to do and me arches falling fast, Mr. Fenton, I sometimes wish as 'ow it was me that was in me grave where there's no more stairs nor slop pails."

I made consoling noises in the back of my throat.

"And I wasn't the only one as knew that there was trouble coming, Mr. Fenton. There was Mr. 'Ankin, too. Unhappy and wretched 'e was, sir, ever since last Monday night when Mr. Baumann was took. Brooding, too, and frightened.

"Why, 'e even forgot to empty Mr. Somerville's coffee pot two nights running and 'e didn't draw Dr. Long's curtains to keep the sunlight off them precious books of 'is. 'E wasn't 'isself, sir. I could see it with me naked heyes though 'e never did say nothing, not being one to talk. And now 'e's took too. Well, well...."

With this dreary reflection she wiped her mouth with her duster and walked a trifle unsteadily from the room. I ran downstairs and found Michael waiting for me. As we passed the porter's lodge, I called the Master's secretary to ask whether, in view of the recent tragedy, we should be expected to attend the tea-party tomorrow. She replied that the invitations had been issued at eleven o'clock that morning and the Master had expressed himself as particularly anxious that the smooth running of college activities should not be interfered with.

Then Michael took me on the step of his bicycle to the upper reaches of the Cam where the boats were busy practicing for the May races. The banks of the river were crowded with brightly dressed boys and girls who were cheering lustily for their favourite crews.

As the boats cut through the water behind the willow trees, Michael and I talked and ragged as we used to in the old days. We called out rude things to the boats that were planning to bump All Saints off the river.

We cheered the Varsity crew as it rowed majestically by, like a proud swan followed by a flock of ugly ducklings. We acted as though nothing serious or tragic had ever happened in our lives. We were like a couple of kids out on a spree who know that there is trouble ahead of them when they get home. But today we did not care.

And so neither of us even mentioned the topic that was uppermost in both our minds.

CHAPTER XIII

Mad Tea Party

THE next day was Sunday and a memorial service was held in the college chapel for Baumann and Hankin. All Saints attended in a body, from the youngest pantry boy to the Master himself, who sat through the service like a figure hewed from the granite of another era.

The Dean preached a moving sermon and when, after the benediction, we all remained standing for Chopin's Funeral March, I am sure that there was not a soul in the chapel who was not mindful of his mortality and grateful for the gift of life which had been snatched so suddenly and so tragically from these two.

I say that the whole college had assembled to pay a last tribute to its dead. Fellows, agnostic and atheist—servants, male and female—undergraduates, Jew and Gentile—all were there. And when I looked round at that sea of faces, I felt a sudden clutching at my throat as I reflected that someone in that vast congregation must be harboring within his breast a terrible and guilty secret.

That someone had knelt in the sight of God with a lie on his lips. He had stood with bowed head in mock reverence towards those whose death he had caused. And no thunderbolt from heaven had descended upon him. But I did not envy him his conscience.

When I came out of chapel, I found that even the weather seemed to reflect the general atmosphere of gloom and depression. It was a cold, dreary day. A thick Scotch mist hung tenaciously over Cambridge and it showed no sign of clearing when I presented myself at the front door of the Master's lodge at four-thirty in the afternoon.

To my surprise it was Mary Smith who answered my ring. Though her face now bore the mask-like composure of the perfect English servant, the traces of yesterday's ordeal were still apparent. I muttered a few conventional words of sympathy as she ushered me into the Master's study. Dr. Warren, Michael, Comstock, Somerville and one or two other undergraduates were already seated stiffly around in a semicircle.

Dr. Hyssop greeted me in his usual affectionate manner, asked after my father and started to chatter so amusingly that his gaiety soon infected his guests and made them forget themselves and the dreary weather. He had evidently decided that the watchword of the college should be "Business as usual during the crisis."

But while we were waiting for tea to be brought in, Dr. Hyssop managed to create a few minor crises in his own inimitable manner, doubtless with a view to diverting our minds from the major one which occupied us all. He began by warmly congratulating Somerville on his success in winning the Lenox Scholarship.

When the slight flutter caused by this remark had subsided, he turned to Michael and said that he had heard of his wonderful performance against the M. C. C. on Thursday. He went on to remark that he considered All Saints to be singularly blest in its blues and brains.

Though he did not mention the fact, it was also singularly blest in having the most original Master in Cambridge. For, during the past eighty or ninety years Dr. Martineau Hyssop had had abundant opportunity to perfect the art of saying the right things to the wrong people.

His little mistakes had made him almost as famous as the much misquoted Dr. Spooner of New College, Oxford. It amounted almost to genius. But he dropped his little bricks so charmingly that they seldom, if ever, fell on sensitive corns. A great deal is forgiven a man who has lived through four or five generations and retained his interest in the things that go on in the world around him.

Still more must be forgiven a man who has always been careful never to say the wrong thing to the right person, which, when all's said and done, is a very different kettle of fish. Whatever his eccentricities, the Master of All Saints will always be my ideal of the perfect type of perfect English gentleman.

The ball of conversation had started to roll smoothly along when Mary appeared bearing a stand of cakes, some hot buttered toast and the diminutive sandwiches which grace the British tea-table more as an ornament than to satisfy hunger. These she placed in front of the fire. The Master was now busy talking to two very young freshmen, one of whom I recognized as the son of the Governor of Senegambia. Both of these youths were hugging the fire in their jejeune shyness and embarrassment.

"A fire is pleasant on a day like this," remarked our host genially. "But it has been so warm recently I didn't think that even my old bones would need any more artificial heat this term."

"It has been very warm," shivered the son of the tropics.

"But not so warm as where *your* father is," said the Master turning politely to the other youth, whose father had been dead for years.

At this juncture Mary appeared again, bearing a large silver teapot which she set reverently on a side table. There was the sound of a distant bell ringing.

The Master rose from his seat and started to busy himself over the tea for which he was so famous among the connoisseurs and which he never allowed anyone but himself to pour. He had barely filled one cup when Mary entered again, this time from the direction of the front door. She announced in clear, matter-of-fact tones:

"Miss Camilla Lathrop."

Dr. Hyssop put down the cup which he had just poured and turned towards the door. I looked round in amazement, hardly able to believe my ears or my eyes. Camilla, dressed in soft, dove-gray, was moving hesitatingly across the room towards her venerable host.

In her left hand she held an engraved invitation card like the one I had received yesterday. Her expression showed that she was not to be damped by the fact that she was the only woman present, but I could tell that beneath this outward poise and assurance she was as nervous as a girl of sixteen.

The Master had bustled over to greet her.

"Delighted, delighted, Miss—Miss—?"

"Lathrop," supplemented Camilla.

"Of course, of course. So nice of you to come, Miss Haytop. Won't you sit here?"

The rest of us, who had been strolling round the room and examining the Master's interesting souvenirs, were then called over and introduced by perfectly good names. The only thing wrong with them was that they did not happen to be our own. After the introductions our host resumed his interrupted occupation of pouring out tea, leaving Dr. Warren to entertain Camilla.

As I watched these two together and noticed the warm, cordial way in which the tutor talked to her, I could not resist a sudden stab of unreasonable jealousy. Though old enough to be her father, he was still a very attractive man. It was obvious that she liked him and also obvious that they were not meeting for the first time.

The glorious profile was glowing with animation and response as she listened and replied. The dark blue eyes were full of intelligent, almost affectionate understanding as they met the serious gaze of Dr. Warren. I was curious and perturbed.

It was a relief when the teacups began to circulate and the Master went back to his place on the couch by Camilla's side. The senior tutor took a cup of tea from Mary's hand and gave it to his neighbour. The nicest looking of the freshmen passed the toast with over-ostentatious alacrity.

Camilla was the pivot around which everyone's solicitude revolved. So far she had not given me so much as a fleeting smile. My nose was completely out of joint, but not to such an extent that I could not appreciate the calm dexterity with which she was handling what would have seemed an exceedingly difficult situation to nine girls out of ten.

Why on earth had the Master elected to invite her to an entirely male tea party? It was obvious that he had never met her before. He did not even know her name! Such a thing must be unique in the annals of an anti-feminist university. It was as fantastic as Alice's sojourn in Wonderland—as improbable as her tea party with the Mad Hatter!

Suddenly the tutor looked up and caught my eye fixed jealously upon him and his neighbour. An extraordinary expression passed over his face. "Mr. Fenton," he said, with his nearest approach to a smile, "we old men must not monopolize the only lady present. Perhaps—"

I glared at him sulkily without moving. But Stuart Somerville had caught the remark and quickly rushed forward to fill the place where at least one angel had feared to tread.

"You are not drinking your tea, Miss Claythorn," I heard the Master say. "You must appreciate my tea, you know. John Masefield told me the other day that I am the only man in England besides himself who really understands the finer points of tea. He got this for me on one of his cruises!"

Camilla raised her cup to her lips. "It has a remarkable bouquet," she said, smiling, "like—er—almond blossoms. I love China tea."

As she spoke, the Master leant forward so suddenly that he almost upset her cup. Very gently he laid one of his wrinkled old hands on Camilla's wrist. A look of pain and bewilderment had come into his mild blue eyes.

"My dear young lady," he said earnestly, "you mustn't, you really must *not* talk about China tea to me. No self-respecting fellow of a Cambridge college ever serves China tea to his guests. To a real tea lover the Chinese product is nothing more or less than decadent dishwater. Now this comes to me specially from Ceylon. It is the finest hand-picked leaf, packed in lead boxes."

Poor Camilla blushed furiously. "I'm sorry," she murmured.

Everyone had stopped talking and was staring at her with a mixture of sympathy and pity. Dr. Warren, evidently suspecting an uncomfortable situation, started a loud conversation in another corner of the room. No one paid much attention to him.

The Master had now taken the cup from her hand and was shaking a finger at her playfully.

"Don't be distressed," he said. "It's quite natural that you—" Here he sniffed delicately at her cup with the flair of a connoisseur. "Why," he cried suddenly, "you are quite right! They must have made some mistake in the kitchen because it *is* China tea! God bless my soul!

"Warren, here is a young lady who knows more about tea than I do. She is that *rara avis,* a woman with a palate—a discriminating sense." He looked at her almost affectionately. "You never learnt anything as useful as this at Girton, my dear. It is a gift—a heaven-sent gift!"

The unfortunate Camilla looked more uncomfortable than ever. Her eyes sought mine in mute appeal but I had no help to offer. Surely the old man must be in his dotage. The atmosphere of the room was stiff with nervous embarrassment. Dr. Hyssop, however, seemed carried away with enthusiasm for his subject.

"Will you please ring the bell, Mr. Somerville. Thank you." The maid appeared.

"Mary," said the Master with mock severity, "through some unfortunate error, China tea has been served today. I thought the household knew that I never use it myself or offer it to my guests. Will you please take the pot away and bring in some of my best Ceylon."

"It is the same as what you always have Sundays," said the girl, blushing apologetically.

"Please do as I say. Cook must have made a mistake. You can take away the cups, too."

Mary took the teapot and collected the cups on a tray. I noticed, however, that the Master retained his own and Camilla's. I also managed to take a hurried sip before my cup was removed.

Now, I am only an American and, as such, cannot be expected to understand the finer points of so essentially British a beverage as tea. But I had been in England almost a year and I did know China tea when I tasted it. As a matter of fact I prefer it, though nothing would have induced me to admit my Philistinism at this moment.

At any rate, I was certain that this was no more China tea than it was bathtub gin. Whether from India or Ceylon I was not prepared to swear, but it was *not* from China—no, definitely no! Again I asked myself what had come over the Master. Was he just making a beautiful gesture to cover Camilla's mistake and his own subsequent lack of tact?

Was he deliberately putting himself in the wrong for some obscure reason of his own? Or was he merely dropping a few more of his characteristic bricks, oblivious of the fact that he was causing a most unpleasant social contretemps?

He had now risen from his seat to place Camilla's cup on the mantelpiece. "Now you shall have some *real* tea, Miss Dunlop," he said smiling and bowing slightly in her direction. "It will be a great privilege to hear the opinion of an expert on my own particular brew." He turned toward me: "And while we are waiting, Hilary, there is something I want to show you. A letter from your father— over here."

I followed him to his desk in the far corner of the room, noting, as I did so, that Stuart lost no time in switching on Camilla the full battery of his charms.

The Master started to fumble among some papers in his desk. He beckoned me closer. "Listen to me very carefully," he whispered. "Can you hear me, Hilary?" I nodded my head. "Well, in a few minutes I am going to clear the room. I am going to be rather impolite and get rid of my guests. I have a reason. Go when the others go, but stay with the young lady. Ask her to return here immediately and come with her. Is that clear?" I nodded again. He handed me a blank sheet of paper. I looked at it with assumed interest. "Here is the letter," he said out loud. "Very, very amusing," I replied, staring unseeingly at its blankness.

We then rejoined the group by the fireplace, where the Master started to talk as though nothing out of the ordinary had happened.

"I am sorry about this little mistake," he said brightly, "but we must stick by the British Empire. We must uphold the great industry of which your father is such a worthy pillar."

This remark was doubtless intended for the son of the Governor of Senegambia. It was addressed to Lloyd who is the only son and heir of a notorious industry known to the public as Comstock's "Comfy-Knicks." The idea of the Master's trying to support this particular article of merchandise was too much for our sense of gravity. A little ripple of merriment ran round the room.

Dr. Martineau Hyssop looked from one to the other. His face had puckered up into a thousand wrinkles like that of a child who is about to cry.

"I'm sorry, gentlemen, but I've—I've—" here he sank into a chair and his white beard fell forward on his chest. "One of my attacks," he murmured. "Warren, Warren—" His voice died away and we all sprang forward. The smiles faded from our faces. Dr. Warren was the first to reach his side.

"Stand back, please," cried the tutor firmly.

The Master raised a valedictory hand. "I think perhaps—"

Dr. Warren nodded towards the door. We were quick to take the hint and left the room one by one to collect in the court outside.

"Poor old Master," said Somerville to Camilla, but I caught her arm and pulled her gently away before she had time to reply. She looked at me in bewilderment.

"Hilary Fenton," she said, "I believe everyone in All Saints is completely dotty. I have never in all my life—"

"Listen, for God's sake listen to me, Camilla," I whispered earnestly. "Something happened in there just now. I don't know what, but there was a crisis of some sort. You and I have got to go back. That attack of the Master's was a put-up job. We must shake the others somehow. Get me?"

"How about finishing this jolly little tea party in my room?" said Stuart with a collective look round him. "I don't serve decadent dishwater." His cornflower eyes rested questioningly on Camilla.

"I'm sorry," she said, "but I have got to get back to Newnham. Mr. Fenton is going with me. Thank you all the same."

We moved off in the direction of the Backs and waited until the little group had dispersed from the vicinity of the Master's lodge. Then we snatched our opportunity and returned.

We found the Master and Dr. Warren in the study where we had left them. Dr. Hyssop had completely recovered from his "attack," but his face was exceedingly grave. A cup of tea was on the table in front of him. Dr. Warren picked it up and passed it to me.

"Mr. Fenton," he said seriously, "you are not a scientist, I know. But perhaps you can tell me what this cup smells of. It is the one which was given to Miss Lathrop a short while ago."

I took the cup from his hand and sniffed at it wonderingly. I have already said that I am peculiarly sensitive to odours. There was no mistake about this one.

"Peaches and almonds," I said unhesitatingly.

The senior tutor nodded. "And do you happen to know what chemical smells like bitter almonds or the kernel of peach stones?"

I searched back in my memory to the early scientific groundings of my prep-school days. A sudden hazy recollection made cold beads of perspiration stand out on my forehead.

"Prussic acid. Oh, my God!"

"Potassium cyanide. Exactly. That is my guess, too, though we cannot be certain until we have made an analysis." Dr. Warren's voice was calm and level. "Unless I am very much mistaken, someone has deliberately tried to kill Miss Lathrop with one of the most deadly and virulent poisons known to man. And that someone would have succeeded had it not been for the extraordinary dexterity of the Master."

Camilla had subsided into a chair and was staring at the two men in horror.

"Poison *me!*" she gasped.

A warm expression of sympathy spread over Dr. Warren's usually impassive face as he looked at her. Once again I had the feeling that there was something between these two—some secret which they shared against the world.

"I'm afraid so, my dear," said the Master gently. "We can come to no other conclusion. Here is my own cup. It is harmless. Hilary, I saw, drank some of his, and the others—well, they are still alive, I presume."

"Good God!" I cried, "this is the most ghastly, the most awful—" I was shaking with rage and excitement.

"Please, Mr. Fenton, keep control of yourself," cut in the cool incisive voice of the tutor. "I have telephoned to Inspector Horrocks. He will be here immediately."

"And I owe you a profound apology," said the Master to Camilla. "Throughout the whole course of my life I have never deliberately caused embarrassment or distress to a lady. I regret to say that my manners this afternoon were execrable.

"But there was nothing else to be done. I knew there was something the matter with your tea as soon as you spoke of almond blossoms. I did not wish to make a scene in front of the young men. I confess I acted clumsily but it was for the best."

"I don't know how to thank you, Master," said Camilla simply. "But you must forgive me for asking you just one question. Why *did* you invite me here today? When your card came this morning—"

The Master had risen from his seat and was looking closely into her eyes. "My dear young lady," he said at length, "it has been a pleasure—a great pleasure and privilege to meet you. I know I am old and absent-minded, so I am sure you will forgive me when I tell you that I did *not* invite you here today.

"The invitation which you received was sent without my knowledge. Indeed, before this afternoon, I had never heard of you in my life. But I sincerely hope that this is only the beginning of a long and pleasant friendship."

CHAPTER XIV

Riddling the Tea Leaves

Following the surprising announcement of the Master's there was a moment of general consternation. It was broken by the arrival of Inspector Horrocks. His florid countenance and large, tangible presence seemed to bring us back from the fantastic realms of Jabberwocky. It was as though an errant ray of sunlight had filtered through the fog which darkened the day. His very feet inspired fresh confidence. Here, at last, was something solid and real.

The detective listened with intelligent interest while Dr. Warren outlined the salient points of the affair. His expression, however, was serious and perplexed as the tutor concluded:

"Of course, I cannot be positive that this cup actually contains prussic acid. It is remotely possible that the whole thing is some kind of unfortunate lark. That the tea had been tampered with is obvious. Pending an analysis, I think we may assume that it is potassium cyanide."

"I'm prepared to take your word for it, Colonel," agreed the Inspector, as he held the cup to his nose. "Smells familiar to me, too."

He turned to the Master. "And now, sir, if you've no objection, I think I shall take down the names of the people who were here today."

Dr. Warren and I supplied the necessary information which was promptly transferred to the inspector's notebook. "Funny how we always seem to get back to 'A' staircase," he murmured, as he scanned the list. "Thank you. Now perhaps Dr. Hyssop would be kind enough to give me some idea of what happened when he poured the tea."

The Master passed a hand reflectively over his beard. "As I recall it," he said slowly, "I had poured out one cup only when the young lady was announced. I was rather up—no, upset is too strong a word. Shall we say that I was pleasantly surprised? I put down the cup and walked across the room to shake hands with my unexpected guest. That took me, at a rough estimate, about two minutes."

"And the others? What were they doing?" asked Horrocks with deference.

The Master looked at me helplessly. "Did you notice what they were doing, Hilary?"

"Yes, Master. While you were welcoming Miss Lathrop the rest of us were wandering about the room, looking at your pictures and souvenirs. Everyone must have gone past that side table where the cup was."

The inspector turned toward me with interest. "You mean, Mr. Fenton, that anyone could have taken this opportunity to doctor up the tea?"

I nodded.

"If that is so," interposed Dr. Warren, "then we have no proof that it was Miss Lathrop for whom the poisoned tea was intended. No one could possibly know that this particular cup would get to her."

Something in the tutor's tone annoyed me to an unreasoning pitch of acerbity. "In America," I commented drily, "it is the custom to serve ladies first. Miss Lathrop was the only lady present. Anyone who was accustomed to polite society could have figured that she would be the natural person to receive the first cup that was poured."

The inspector looked at me with an expression of amused approbation. "And was it the maid who gave her the cup?" he inquired.

Dr. Warren screwed his monocle into place and looked his ex-sergeant squarely in the eyes.

"No, I regret to say that I myself handed it to Miss Lathrop. The maid passed the back of the sofa with two cups in her hand. I took the nearest and naturally passed it on."

"H'mm. Then we have no actual proof that it was the first cup to be poured that the young lady received. In view, however, of her extraordinary invitation, I think we may take it that she was the intended victim." The inspector paused and cleared his throat. "Did you leave the side table again while you were pouring out, Dr. Hyssop?"

"No," replied the Master. "After I had left Miss Lathrop next to Dr. Warren on the sofa, I poured out the rest of the cups and went back to join them."

"And what happened next?"

"The next thing I remember is that Dr. Warren left the sofa and offered me his seat," I said as casually as I could.

"Did you take it?"

"No. Somerville went over and sat by Miss Lathrop. She was between him and the Master when she made her remark about the China tea."

"Yes, yes," agreed the Master, "and such a fortunate—such a very fortunate remark it was. As soon as she mentioned almonds, I knew that something was amiss."

Horrocks puffed out his enormous moustache. "And did anyone else come up to Miss Lathrop at this time—that is, near enough to slip anything into her cup?"

"Several people came over to pass her the toast, the cakes or something of that sort," replied Dr. Warren, "but I did not see anyone standing near her for any length of time."

"I see. Then as a matter of actual fact, we cannot be at all certain as to when or how the poison was administered," commented the inspector. "One thing seems to be certain, however, and that is that no one acted in a manner to create suspicion. Am I right?"

There was no reply. Horrocks then turned to Camilla, who had been sitting still throughout the whole conversation with her chin resting on one hand. Once again she reminded me of a marble figure, magnificently impervious to all that was unpleasant or unlovely in the world around her.

"Perhaps, Miss, you would be so kind as to tell me something more about this strange invitation you received."

"I really have very little to tell," she said reluctantly. "I am as completely mystified as the rest of you. I was in my room at about twelve o'clock this morning when a girl called Dorothy Dupuis brought me Dr. Hyssop's card. She said she had found it in the hall.

"I asked the porter but he did not know anything about it. It had obviously been delivered by hand—and quite recently. Of course, I thought it a little odd and that the invitation should be for the same day, but I didn't attach much importance to that. I was so pleased and flattered to be invited by Dr. Hyssop. I've often heard of him, naturally, and I wanted to meet him.

"So I came, and you know the rest. With the exception of Mr. Fenton, whom I know slightly, there was no one here whom I had ever seen before. I know Mr. Somerville by reputation, as a cricketer. I saw him play the other day.

"And—and Dr. Warren—" She broke off and looked earnestly at the serious faces in front of her. "But it is quite inconceivable that anyone should have wanted to poison me. Nor can I imagine why anyone should have tried to get me here with a forged invitation."

"Do you happen to have that card with you, Miss?" asked the Inspector.

Camilla produced from her bag the small square of cardboard; engraved with the All Saints crest, which informed her that the Master requested the pleasure of her company to tea at four-thirty o'clock that afternoon. The name, Miss Camilla Lathrop, had been filled in by typewriter, also the time and the date of the party.

"It is one of my regular cards," commented the Master. "I have a number of them in my office. But, as a rule, my secretary fills them in by hand."

Horrocks nodded. "May I see your typewriter, please, sir?" he asked.

We followed the Master into his secretary's office. He pointed to the machine on the desk. "It's an old model Underhill," he explained, "but that won't be much help as almost every typewriter in the college is the same make and the same—er—vintage.

"I don't know anything about those that are privately owned, of course. But the college bought about a dozen of these some three years ago when the company either changed their model or went out of business. I remember that we got them very cheap. Isn't that so, Warren?"

The senior tutor nodded.

By this time the inspector had slipped a piece of paper into the machine and tapped out "Miss Camilla Lathrop. Tea. 4:30pm" several times.

"It's the same type," he remarked, after he had compared it with the invitation card. "But it might have been done on this or any of the Underhills that had a black ribbon. None of these letters is broken or defaced in any way so as to distinguish them. I will examine some of the others later. I suppose," he added with some diffidence, "there is no chance of your secretary's having made a mistake?"

"My secretary," replied the Master, "is a very efficient young woman. She does not make mistakes, and she would not dream of sending out a personal invitation that had been filled in with the typewriter. I gave her a list of names yesterday morning. I invited all the people who live on 'A' staircase for reasons of my own.

"Indirectly they have all been involved in the two terrible tragedies that have occurred lately. I wanted to see them for myself. But under no circumstances would I have invited a single young lady to a party composed solely of men. In some respects I am old fashioned.

"Or, perhaps, by now the circle has gone round and I am in fashion again. It has made so many revolutions since my young days." He looked around him with a bland smile. "However, I will call my secretary, if you like—just to make sure."

He lifted the receiver and gave a number. A clear, efficient voice replied:

"Indeed, no, Master, I always fill them in by pen. Yes, you gave me the list at ten-thirty yesterday morning. There was no lady's name. Most of the young gentlemen were on 'A' staircase. Yes, I am quite sure. Good-bye."

"Well, that leaves us, like you might say, just about where we were before," commented the inspector, as we returned to the Master's study.

Dr. Martineau Hyssop seated himself in his favourite chair and held his shrivelled hands out toward the fire. The benevolent countenance was clouded and weary. He looked cold and pinched.

"I simply can't believe it," he whispered. "In all my long life—at my own tea-party—poison—a charming young girl—" the old voice drifted away dispiritedly.

The military tones of Horrocks cut through his dying monologue. "There's one thing we ought to look into, Colonel, and that is what you might call the source of supply. I wonder, now, where anyone could get hold of prussic acid here in the college."

The tutor seemed to reflect for a moment. "There is—or was—some in my science laboratory," he said at length.

"Where's that?"

"It's just off my rooms on 'A' staircase. I give my lectures there sometimes and use it for practical demonstrations with my students. Hankin used to look after it and keep it clean. It was one of his regular jobs. As a rule, he kept the place locked, but it's just possible that since his death—" A sudden thought seemed to strike him. "I think I'll go over and see. I won't be a moment."

Dr. Warren left the room and returned in a few minutes carrying in his hand a half-empty bottle labelled "Potassium Cyanide (KCN) *poison*." The lines round his mouth looked deeper than usual.

"There doesn't seem to be much doubt as to what you call the source of supply, Horrocks," he said grimly. "At the beginning of last week this bottle was full. I have used none since that time. It looks as if someone had been helping himself pretty freely. And he's taken enough to kill several people."

The inspector took the bottle and removed the stopper. As I moved toward him, I noticed an odour suggesting oil of bitter almonds. "I wouldn't smell that too closely," warned the tutor, drily. "It gives off hydrocyanic acid gas, which won't do you any good."

"There's not much need to do that," answered Horrocks, as he restoppered the bottle. "It's easy enough to tell now what was in that cup!" He addressed the Master in grave tones.

"Dr. Hyssop," he said quietly, "I've seen enough to be convinced that someone in this room today deliberately attempted to commit a murder." A look of understanding passed between him and Dr. Warren. He resumed. "Both Dr. Warren and I have very good reason to believe that Miss Lathrop was the intended victim. I think that she herself—"

"I know what you mean," interposed the Master gently. "But isn't even that rather fantastic?"

"The plain facts are before you, sir," said the inspector, pointing to the cup and bottle. "Now there remains the important question of motive."

Camilla had jumped up from her chair and was looking anxiously around her. When she spoke, her voice was low and tense.

"Don't!" she cried, "please don't go into that. Not here—not in front of me—or Hilary. He doesn't know about it. And I've had all that I can stand. I want to go—please."

Everyone was looking at her compassionately. I would never have believed that Dr. Warren's face could be so gentle. He came over and laid his hand on her shoulder.

"Yes, yes, Miss Lathrop," he said. "We all understand. You are quite right. It would be better for you to go. Mr. Fenton, I am sure, will be glad to go with you. And, perhaps, if you feel like it, you would come to my room in about an hour's time. There are one or two things—yes?"

Camilla turned blindly towards the door. Then, as if she had suddenly remembered her manners, she went over to the Master and held out her hand.

"Good-bye, Dr. Hyssop," she said simply, "and thank you. I'm sorry to have been such a nuisance to you."

The Master took her hand between both of his and looked up into her glistening eyes.

"My dear," he said softly, "I would not have had this happen for anything in the world. Now that I know more about you, I shall make it my duty to protect you from any unpleasantness that may come to you through no fault of your own. I want you always to look upon me as your friend.

"You have acted splendidly throughout the whole miserable business. If what has happened today, if the two tragic events of the past week have undermined my belief in human nature, you have helped to restore my confidence in the essential goodness and courage of my fellow beings.

"Will you come and see me tomorrow so that I can tell you how much I have admired you—not only for your conduct today but for other things, too? At about four o'clock? You can bring my young friend, Hilary, with you, if you wish. And now, good-bye, my dear. Good-bye and God bless you."

He accompanied us to the front door and we passed out into the misty atmosphere of the court. I took Camilla's arm and my eyes sought hers.

"Let's go up to my room," I whispered. "You are tired and overwrought. I won't worry you to talk. You shall just listen to me."

"All right, Hilary Fenton," she agreed wearily.

When we reached "A" staircase both of us instinctively looked back toward the Master's lodge. By some strange trick of vision we could see that Dr. Hyssop was still standing by the front door. Only his white beard was visible, but that seemed to pierce the fog like a beacon light—a patch of pure whiteness against the gray obscurity of the day. The sight comforted me strangely.

"He's like a guardian angel," I murmured.

"He's my idea of God," said Camilla with decision.

CHAPTER XV

Family History

THE first thing I did, after returning to my room, was to light a fire and draw the curtain. It was a relief to shut out the cold, dreary day—to anticipate the night by creating darkness artificially—to watch the firelight flicker over Camilla's pale face and to feel that I was shut in with her, warm and cosy in a private little world of our own.

It was now too late for tea and toast. A bottle of brandy (much depleted by Comstock and Mrs. Bigger) was all that I had to offer. Camilla was adamant in refusing, so I was obliged to commit what to all rightminded Englishmen is the only unforgivable sin— to drink spirits before the official setting of the sun. I felt, however, that the occasion demanded something drastic. The Master's tea party had reduced me to a state of pulp.

After I had completed my medical potations, I went across and sat on the sofa by Camilla. I took her cold hand in mine and for a few minutes stayed perfectly still without daring to speak. I could not tell whether she was even conscious of my presence. But I did not care. For the first time in my life I was completely happy.

Suddenly, however, she sat up with a little start and looked at her wrist watch. A slow smile spread over her face.

"Only forty minutes before I have to go down to Dr. Warren's rooms. You'd better hurry up and ask some of those questions, Hilary Fenton. I know you're bursting with them."

She had not withdrawn her hand.

"I haven't any questions to ask," I whispered, "except one: and I'll go on asking that all my life until you give me the right answer."

Almost imperceptibly she shook her head, but there was a promise in her eyes. All the thoughts and images she had evoked in my mind during the past week now rushed to my lips for expression.

"Camilla," I said, as our faces drew nearer together, "I wish I could talk with tongues. I would tell you that you are like all the best things I've ever seen or heard in my life. You make me think of the light of a sunset reflected on the breast of a seagull—the dogwoods in Valley Forge—the opening chorus of Swinburne's *Atalanta*—the smell of migonette—"

But Camilla had pulled her hand away and was covering up her ears.

"Please, Hilary Fenton," she cried, "I can't bear that kind of thing now. It's very beautiful and you are a dear, but not now. I want you to be absolutely sincere with me. Anyone who had a little imagination or—" here she smiled almost roguishly "—or who happened to be reading English literature, could talk that way. But just at this moment I'm lonely. I'm miserable. I feel an outcast. I want solid ground under my feet. I want—I don't know what I want, but it's not poetry."

I rose from the couch and stood in the Englishman's favourite attitude with my back to the fire. We looked into each other's eyes without smiling.

"Speech, my dear," I said at length, "was given us so that we could conceal our thoughts. I talk a lot of nonsense, I know. But I can't hide the big, fundamental and ridiculously simple things that I am thinking. You know perfectly well that I love you and want to marry you. I've always loved you—years before I even met you.

"It's not the springtime nor just a young man's fancy. It's the real thing. I'll admit frankly that you haven't made me miss any meals, except possibly my tea today, but you've kept me from looking at or thinking of other girls for a whole week. You've given me something I've never had in my life before."

"But, Hilary, that's nothing—nothing at all. It's happening in Cambridge all the time. Boys and girls are attracted to each other. They make fine speeches. They fall in love at lunch over lamb chops on Monday and they separate forever on Thursday afternoon over walnut cake and sundaes at Fuller's. Life's been pretty grim for me. I can't play. I can't even pretend. Lots of people have talked that way to me. Men do it to almost any girl who isn't positively hideous."

"In other words, Miss Lathrop, you think it's just that Græco-Roman profile of yours that I am in love with. That Doric nose; that Byzantine chin. Well, let me tell you I'll love you even better when you have seven chins and seven babies—and I hope they'll all be mine. The chins and the babies, I mean.

"I love you in spite of the awful mackintosh you wear, that unspeakable bicycle you ride. I love everything about you. The Devonshire cream in your voice—the little mousetrap which goes snap, snap in your mind—your manners to older people—and the fact that you can sit down and stand up without showing your—"

I paused and looked at her. To my surprise her eyes were wet like forget-me-nots under the water. She was making frantic efforts to get at a handkerchief.

"Camilla, darling," I cried, and as she lifted her mouth to mine, I could feel her trembling like a child. For awhile we remained thus without speaking.

"And now," I cried exultantly, "the only thing we have to decide is whether you can bear the thought of living in America—for a while, at any rate. Philadelphia isn't a bad place and it's quite close to Atlantic City."

She held up her hand to silence me. "No, Hilary, I—"

"All right, we'll live in England—in Timbuctu—in Guatemala, I don't care. I've got a little money of my own. I'll buy a shack in the Andes or in Alaska."

Camilla had now risen from her chair and walked across the room. She took a cigarette from the box on the table and puffed it gloomily. Presently she spoke:

"Don't you think you've talked long enough, Hilary Fenton? Your nonsense is very charming, my dear, but it's about your turn to listen to mine for awhile. And mine is anything but charming— nor is it nonsense, unfortunately. Of course, if I married you, I wouldn't care where we lived. In fact, I'd love to get out of England, but I'm afraid I am not going to marry you."

"Then you are not going to get any peace this side of the grave," I cried excitedly.

"I am not going to marry you," she said, throwing her cigarette into the fire, "and I'm not going to marry you for the simple reason that you ... are ... not ... going ... to want ... to marry ... me."

Her face had gone strangely and suddenly gray. She walked back to the couch. I tried to laugh reassuringly but there was a cold, clammy feeling in the pit of my stomach. I started to speak.

"Hilary," she cried, "do please listen to me and don't try to be funny any more. I do want to talk to you seriously. I had hoped you would ask me questions about today—about what happened at tea—why the Master said what he did. It would have made it so much easier."

"Consider all the questions asked," I replied gently.

"Then you really want to hear about me? You know so little, you see, and—and I don't want to be dramatic about it—but there is so much."

I nodded. "Begin with the birds and the flowers, my dear. I bet you were a beautiful baby."

As I lit a cigarette and arranged myself comfortably on the couch, I felt her hand on my sleeve.

"No," she said, "I won't begin at the beginning. I'll come back to that later on. First of all I want to tell you about my family life. About my father. You've heard of Lathrop of Bristol?"

I nodded again. "Yes, Dorothy Dupuis told me your people were as rich as Croesus and that King George took it as a personal affront when you refused to be presented at Court."

Camilla smiled. "How funny it sounds when it's put that way. As a matter of fact, Hilary, my father—that is, Mr. Lathrop—is rich, but it doesn't mean anything to me. He has cut me off. I don't get anything from him at all. I don't even go to him in the holidays. Fortunately I don't have to because my mother left me a small income when she died.

"Last year, when I was twenty-one, I went to my father and told him that my ambition was to go to Newnham. I was tired of leading a so-called social life in Clifton. I hate the place with its silly women quarrelling like cats over their wretched threepenny bridge—with its interminable crocodiles of school girls. Have you ever seen a crocodile, Hilary Fenton?"

"No, but I'm like Hamlet in that I'm prepared to eat one—under certain circumstances, of course!"

"Well, when I presented my ultimatum, my father told me that he had other plans for me. I knew just exactly what those plans were and we quarrelled. He is obstinate and cold. He can see no point of view but his own. He has never cared about me particularly except as an instrument to promote his own particular schemes. Finally I asked him to give me at least one good reason why I should not go to Cambridge with my own money. It was then that the storm broke."

Camilla paused and looked at me anxiously. I pressed her hand.

"This is hard to say, Hilary Fenton. You've got to be very sympathetic or I can't go on." I squeezed her hand again and raised it to my lips. She turned her head away from me and continued, addressing the far corner of the room.

"Then Mr. Lathrop—I can't call him father—lost his temper with me completely. He called me a charity brat, a waif, a—oh, I don't know what he said, but I learnt then, for the first time that I was not really his daughter. That Mrs. Lathrop, whom I had adored, was not my real mother. I had been adopted by her after the death of their own child.

"Her money, so he said, had come to me under false pretenses. The name of Lathrop merely covered the shame and disgrace of my own family. I was nothing but the daughter of a criminal—a notorious homicidal lunatic. In short, Hilary, I am not Camilla Lathrop at all, I am—my real name is ... is ... Corinne North."

She had turned toward me and her eyes were looking searchingly into mine as though she was trying to bore a hole through my brain. It was one of those moments when the fate of a lifetime—two lifetimes—hangs in the balance. I threw my arms about her.

"My dear, my dear," I stammered, "as if I cared about that. You are you and that's all that really matters. Besides, Corinne North is a beautiful name. It's much prettier than Camilla Lathrop. I love you all the more. I don't give a damn about your family. When all's said and done, only God can make a family tree and I'm rather proud of yours. I've met your father. He's a dear. I like him. I'd be delighted to have him for a father-in-law. Now, don't cry, darling."

I wiped her eyes and after a moment she continued.

"But, quite apart from the tragedy of my father, there were other reasons why he—Mr. Lathrop—did not want me to come up to Cambridge. He told me that he had been given to understand that I had a brother up here. He did not wish us to meet each other and revive the old family scandal.

"William North, as perhaps you know, had two children. One of them was adopted by the Lathrops—that was myself. The other was a boy about a year older than I. His name was Jules. He was adopted by a rich South African farmer named Baumann."

I sat up suddenly. "Great heavens! Then Julius Baumann was your brother. Oh, you poor kid!"

She nodded. "Yes, he was my brother. As I told you before, I met him when I first came up to Cambridge. I sought him out of my own free will and against Mr. Lathrop's wishes. But he need not have worried about anything coming of it. I found that poor Julius was terribly sensitive about his parentage. It seemed to prey on his mind all the time.

"That was why he was always so anxious to pass for a real South African of Dutch extraction. I believe he hated me for reminding him of—well, at any rate, we agreed that we had better keep apart. You see he was firmly convinced that his—my father was a desperate criminal and a dangerous maniac. I could not agree with him."

"He was wrong on that score," I cried. "William North is a scholar and a gentleman if ever I saw one."

"Well, whatever the truth about father, I realized that it was impossible for Julius and me to be friends. I never saw him again until the day I met you. After that Blake lecture I happened to see a newspaper and read that William North had escaped.

"I hurried around to Julius' rooms. I found him in a dreadful state. He was convinced that father would try to do him some mischief—that he would be involved in some hideous catastrophe. Also, he worried about our mother."

"Your mother? Is she alive?"

"Yes, and I believe she lives somewhere near Cambridge. After the trial she went to Canada with another man. Julius wouldn't tell me anything more about her except that he promised to provide for her financially. I don't even know what name she goes under, but I imagine she has sunk pretty low, poor thing."

"I bet the letter I posted on Monday night was to her," I remarked. "It had money in it. I wish I had looked at the address, then we might be able to trace her, I saw only B-R-I-D-G-E-S on the envelope. I thought it might be the name of a place; I see now it was probably just part of Cam*bridge*shire."

"Anyhow, I'm glad you did post it. Poor Julius was worried to death about her and about himself. You see, he was sure that my father had some sinister purpose—"

"His only purpose was to get into a decent library and look up some sixteenth century books."

"Yes, in my own mind I've always been sure of his innocence. But you can understand now what a terrible shock it was to me when you told me that Julius had been *murdered*. Suicide would not have surprised me much—he was in such an unbalanced state of mind when I saw him last Monday—but murder! You see, I couldn't be sure."

"You poor, poor kid," I murmured. "It must have been hell. I see it all so much more clearly now than I did before. You have explained such a lot of things. But I do wish you'd tell me where you went that day after you left Baumann's rooms. I hung out of the window for half an hour just to see you cross the court."

The shadow of a smile passed over Camilla's face for a moment, then she said seriously:

"I went into Dr. Warren's rooms. He was my father's greatest friend here in All Saints. He knew about me and Julius. I wanted to ask him about my mother, but he knew nothing of her. He was awfully kind. He said he'd let me know if there was any news. He still believes in my father."

"Yes," I said gently, "he believes in him to the extent of sheltering him in his rooms and giving him clothes and money. You know Camilla, I am practically certain that your father was on the staircase the night that Baumann was killed. Of course he had a perfect alibi for the time of Hankin's death, but—"

"Oh, he didn't do it," cried Camilla, "I'm sure he didn't do it. There is someone else—some stranger who hates us all. Someone who knew about Julius and me and who hates us because we are Norths. It was this same person who killed both Julius and Hankin ... Julius because he hated him and Hankin because he knew too much ... the same person who put prussic acid in my tea this afternoon."

"It was the man who spoke to Hankin in the court the night he was killed. They haven't found him yet, but they will, dear. He must have been at the tea party today. The field is getting narrower and narrower. In the meantime, you have got to take care of yourself. I only wish I could protect you against this invisible enemy. You mustn't trust anyone. I don't even want you to go down to Dr. Warren's rooms."

She glanced hurriedly at her wrist watch. "Heavens, I'm late now. I must go. I'll see you tomorrow afternoon at the Master's. Apparently he knows the worst about me too. In the meantime—"

"In the meantime, I shall be loving you even more than ever. I don't care who or what you are. If ever you doubt me, remember that I loved you even when I thought you had taken the law into your own hands with regard to Baumann's death; I loved you when you packed me a wallop on the jaw. I—oh, Camilla, you darling."

For one moment I held her in my arms. "Till tomorrow," she whispered, "and thank you, Hilary, thank you for being so decent about everything."

The next thing I knew was that she had gone.

As I heard her footsteps on the staircase, I reflected on several things. Her story had been a revelation, of course. It had thrown light on several dark places. It had altered several possibilities and perspectives; but it had not brought the main problem any nearer to solution.

As a matter of fact, when I came to think it over, I realized that it had merely made things more diabolically complicated than ever.

CHAPTER XVI

Echoes from the Past

That evening, after leaving Hall, I decided that I must gird up my mental loins and get to work on the new complications which Camilla's story had brought to light. The problem now presented a very different aspect.

Whereas, in the first place, it had seemed as though the available facts were insufficient to make a complete picture, I now felt that there was not enough room in my jigsaw puzzle to fit in all the pieces that I had in my possession. And, at the same time, these facts were singularly lacking in balance or cohesion.

There were, for example, a surprising number of potential murderers—a fair sprinkling of opportunities for them to commit their crimes—but, as far as one could see with the naked eye, no earthly or unearthly motive why anyone should wish to kill three perfectly harmless human beings.

But Camilla had brought out two important points. Money and family relationships were involved—factors which, if properly juggled around and manipulated into place, might easily produce the missing motive. It was to the hunting of this elusive snark that I decided to dedicate myself that evening.

I would begin with William North. He, I felt certain, was the cornerstone of the whole miserable edifice. His crime, tragedy or moment of madness was the focal point about which all things revolved—the *fons et origo mali* from which had sprung these ramifications, past and present. And since I could not study William North in the flesh, I would read up about him in my father's book, which I could borrow from Stuart. Like the answer to a maiden's prayer, Somerville accosted me just as I reached the foot of "A" staircase. He was magnificently dressed and bound, so he said, for a quiet game of poker in Jesus.

"Somerville," I said casually, "there is a little book which I seem to have heard you mention from time to time. I'd like to borrow it from you, if you don't mind. The name, I believe, is *Famous Second Trials.* I think it—"

"Sure thing—you bet—okay, gate," replied Stuart, giving a tolerable imitation of Jerry Colonna's talkie accent. "It's bully reading for a quiet Sunday evening at home. By a wise guy called Fenton. Come into my shack."

He produced a battered copy of my father's volume and turned over its pages with mock reverence.

"I may have to charge you extra for the illustrations," he said solemnly. "Here, for example, is the portrait of the artist as an old man—Fenton *ipse,* complete with wig and robes."

My father had been portrayed with enormous side-whiskers, large spectacles and flowing garments which were reminiscent of the Winged Victory. His appearance had not been improved by the addition of a large wasp, wart or wen to the extreme tip of an extraordinarily Semitic nose.

"My father," I remarked drily, "is fifty-two years old. He is clean shaven and looks rather like the late Sir Gerald du Maurier. He never wears a wig, and I know of no wasp in the world that would have the impertinence to sting the end of his nose. Otherwise your resemblance is excellent."

"Thank you, thank you, Fenton. And how is this for a portrait of Oscar—naughty Mr. Wilde in the act of bursting?" He turned to a picture so horrible that it defies description. "Or, this one of William North, dragging his victim down 'A' staircase by her hair?

"These are my jewels." He paused and lifted his eyes piously heavenward. "Oh, Fenton, Fenton, had I but served my God with half the zeal that I put into these illustrations during lecture hours, I would not have been ploughed in my Mays next month."

I took the book from his hand. "Thank you, Stuart. You are quite an artist. Now run along to Jesus. I will treat this masterpiece as it deserves."

He put a restraining arm on my sleeve.

"No, no, my Hilary. The drains are sensitive. They too have their little feelings. And, by the same token, how is the Old Pill?"

"Better, I believe. His attack was not so serious as it looked."

"Well, he gave you an opportunity to walk your baby back home like a perfect little American knight—without the K. And say, when you are through with that wench, you might—"

But I did not stop for more. With a hurried good night I ran up to my rooms, sported my oak and prepared to spend a profitable hour or two with the only one of my father's books that I had ever opened.

For some little time I waded through a morass of legal technicalities which were just so much Sanskrit to me. Finally, however, as I read on, a picture of William North began to emerge— a picture which in no way resembled the realistic sketch drawn by Somerville in the margin of the book.

I saw a man who had been tried and condemned to death for a crime which he undoubtedly had committed. I saw him fighting what looked like a losing battle after the case had been sent back for retrial, due to some technical misdirection to the jury.

I saw how his friends had stood by him—how they had sworn to his insanity, his unbalanced genius, his nervous temperament which, at the time of the crime, had been superimposed on a state of definite ill health. I saw the astuteness of his counsel in using the man's weakness to strengthen his defense.

I saw how it was possible to juggle slightly yet delicately with the impervious bulwark of the English legal system. I saw the shadow of the gallows gradually begin to fade—to be replaced by the walls of the insane asylum. Even the stiff, textbook phraseology could not altogether rob the case of its drama.

So much for North. But now it was not he alone in whom I was interested. My father had thrown into relief other aspects and other personalities. I was struck by the evidence of Dr. Reginald Warren, then a young man who had just received his fellowship at All Saints.

I was amazed at the coolness with which he had declared his own best friend to be temporarily insane and consequently not responsible for his actions. I was interested in the measured testimony of Dr. Martineau Hyssop, Master of All Saints, who, in his own conservative manner, did as much as anyone for his young colleague. I could see Cambridge presenting a united front against the invasion of its sacred precincts by a hideous chimera.

The figure of Mrs. North was hazy, but I studied it with particular care. At the first trial, it seemed, she had been present with her two infants (Camilla's first public appearance, I reflected bitterly) obviously with a view to gaining for her husband the sympathies of the jury. At the second trial, which took place some months later, she had been absent, as my father put it, "for family reasons."

On the other side of the picture, however, there was the family of the girl whom North had killed. By a strange coincidence her name had happened to be the same as that of one of the greatest comediennes of her day—and perhaps of all days—Marie Lloyd. This was possibly one of the factors which had made the case of such wide popular appeal. The vindictiveness of the Lloyd family struck me particularly. "Blood for our blood" was written in every line of the testimony they gave. They were, as far as I could see, unbending and implacable.

Such, briefly, were the facts and figures most intimately connected with the North scandal. The rest is common knowledge and as well known, even to the layman, as the retribution which finally overtook such arch-criminals as Crippen, Landru and Smith. But with these three, their misdeeds had terminated decently upon the gallows.

With North, it seemed, the evil he had done lived after him—to break out twenty years later like some malignant cancer in the lives of his children. Where in this tangled history of the past could I find a motive to account for these present tragedies?

The most obvious and immediate conclusion, of course, was that the dead girl's family might still be harboring against the North clan a spirit of revenge and hatred—an Old Testament vendetta reaching down to the second and third generation. But why?

North had suffered. He had paid for his crime in full. What was there to choose between death on the gallows and the death-in-life of the asylum? And Marie Lloyd had been in her grave for a long, long time. Her parents were probably in their graves, too. At any rate it was certain that they were not up at Cambridge.

Was it reasonable to suppose that they had bequeathed to their children or grandchildren the undying spirit of hatred towards the Norths? Had this fire smouldered for twenty years, to break out at last on "A" staircase? Revenue without profit in a so-called Christian era? Was that a motive to be taken seriously? Surely there is a limit to human vindictiveness.

But Mrs. North? That dim figure conjured up all sorts of sinister possibilities. She suggested innumerable motives. It was a known fact that she had benefited through the death of her son Jules, alias Julius Baumann. Camilla, too, had money of her own. And—here a fantastic notion crossed my mind—Mrs. North had been a barmaid, so often a first step towards becoming a college bedmaker.

Mrs. Bigger had been a barmaid—Mrs. Fancher's husband owned a public house. Was it possible that Mrs. North had not gone to Canada at all—that she had stayed in Cambridge, nursing her secret schemes against her own flesh and blood? No, the idea was altogether too wild and farfetched. She would have been recognized immediately by Dr. Warren, the Master—anyone who had happened to be present at North's first trial.

She would have been the first person suspected by those who knew. She was a marked character, a branded sheep. As the murderess of her son and the would-be murderess of her daughter she was out of the question. But as I sat there with the book on my knee, I began to play more and more with the idea of Mrs. North. I turned over the pages and read every reference that was made to her.

Suddenly my eye caught once again that phrase—"Mrs. North was absent from the second trial *for family reasons.*" The words fascinated me. It was the only sentence in the whole chapter which seemed to be lacking in the frankness and lucidity which marked my father's textbook style. I read it over again and again.

Then all at once, there flashed into my mind an idea which was eventually to prove almost my only real contribution to the solution of the case. What were the family reasons which could keep Mrs. North from so important an event as the second trial of her husband?

I could see my father nervously shuffling his feet at the breakfast table when my mother asked him some question which involved either the seamy side of human nature or the biological functions of life. Into the phrasing of his one sentence I read paternal embarrassment and paternal delicacy. In short, Mrs. North must have stayed away *because she was expecting another baby!*

At last light seemed to be dawning on me in all directions. Immediately my interest shifted from Mrs. North to the problematic person whom I now began to call North Junior in my mind. The son, presumably, of William North, born, as one might almost say, posthumously to his wife. This son, conceived in shame and despair, gestated during this frightful period of his mother's life, delivered into a world which rang with his father's notorious name.

The other North children, adopted as they were immediately after the tragedy, might well have escaped the taint. But North Junior had been born out of the very bowels of the tragedy itself. Anything might reasonably be expected of such a son. The gall and wormwood that had been bred into the very bones must some day come out in the flesh. He, too, was a marked sheep—but branded secretly with the black mark of God rather than of man. He could run with the flock unnoticed.

And apart from his fearful heredity, there would have been other, more material reasons, why North Junior might wish evil to his brother and sister. Supposing he had been adopted by someone less prosperous than the Lathrops or the Baumanns? Or supposing he had followed the devious fortunes of his mother.

Would not the comparative affluence of Jules and Corinne naturally rankle in his twisted mind? Would he not perhaps hope to inherit some share of the personal fortune which had come to them? Legal quirks aside, was he not one of the next of kin—the logical person to share with his mother any money left by his brother or sister on their death?

"On their death"—and why not, therefore, hasten on that death? I could picture North Junior scheming it all out in his brain— that brain which combined the inherited brilliance of a great scholar and the cunning of an ambitious barmaid. "Hasten on their death!" First Jules, his older brother, then Hankin who had seen or heard something that he had not dared to tell. And then Camilla. After that—who knows?—perhaps his mother would fall a victim, unless she were conniving at his crimes and sharing the spoils. Nothing would have seemed impossible to North Junior. I was beginning to visualize him more clearly now.

I could almost see him standing in the room beside me. He

was taking corporeal shape before my mind's eye. He would, I reflected, be about twenty years old. He might be in his first or second year at Cambridge. He would be approximately the same age as, say, Lloyd Comstock, Stuart Somerville, Michael Grayling or either of the two freshmen who had been at the Master's tea party that day.

Young North was now beginning to obsess me and permeate me completely. I had—I must have met him, talked to him, possibly shaken him by the hand. He was in the college—he was an undergraduate at All Saints like myself. A serpent in the academic garden; a lunatic far more criminal and far more dangerous than his father.

I got up and started to pace the room. I must talk to someone about him, about his mother. I must talk to someone who knew. I should go mad if I didn't share my suspicions with someone. But who? Michael. No, he might be ... Comstock? Oh God! The Master? He was too old and had been sufficiently upset for one day.

Then suddenly I thought of Dr. Warren. I must see him. He knew more about the North family than I did—more about William North than my father—more, probably than any man living.

Breathless with excitement, I ran down to the senior tutor's rooms. I found him seated at his desk, working. He barely looked up when I entered.

"Dr. Warren, I must speak to you, I must—" I stammered out the purpose of my visit.

The eye without the monocle stared at me stonily. "Mr. Fenton, you are disturbing yourself unduly and you are disturbing me. I do not see any reason why you should take these tragedies to yourself exclusively. You have wasted a great deal of time lately in worrying over things that are being investigated by the proper authorities. And, incidentally, speaking of wasted time, I feel it my duty to remind you—as your tutor—that you will have examinations to pass next month."

"I wanted to talk to you, sir, as a human being, not as a tutor," I shouted, flinging respect to the winds. "I am taking things upon myself for a very good reason—because I happen to be in love with Camilla Lathrop—or, if you like it better, with Corinne North, the daughter of the man who was in your rooms, on *this* staircase, the night Jules North, or Julius Baumann, was murdered. I'm taking things upon myself because I am not prepared to stand idly by and see the girl I hope to marry killed in cold blood."

My voice had cracked on a shrill squeak. I knew that I was making myself ridiculous, that I was behaving like a second-rate boor, but I didn't care. Dr. Warren could send me down tomorrow if he wanted to, but tonight I was going to have my say.

Instead of saying it, however, I subsided into the nearest chair. Finally I recovered my breath and glared belligerently at the tutor. There was an expression of surprise rather than anger on his face. Suddenly he rose slowly from his seat and walked across the room towards me.

To my amazement he was holding out his hand. "Fenton," he said, and for the first time he dropped the ceremonious mister, "I apologize. You undoubtedly have the right to be interested. I did not know that you were even acquainted with Miss Lathrop. Perhaps you will allow me to congratulate you on your excellent taste."

I shook his proffered hand weakly.

"I apologize, too, sir," I said, "for bursting in this way. But I had to talk to you. I've just been reading my father's account of the North trial—" Here I explained as briefly as possible some of the results of my evening's occupation. Dr. Warren listened attentively. Finally he spoke:

"Since you have been so frank with me about your suspicions, Fenton, I will tell you something about Monday night—something which I had hoped would remain a secret between Horrocks and myself. It will clear your mind on one point at least. When I returned to my rooms after Hall that evening I found William North here playing my piano.

"He was, as you doubtless know, one of my closest friends at college. My room was the logical place for him to come to in his emergency. We had a long talk, but I never left him alone the whole evening until—well, it would have been impossible for him to have killed Baumann even if the idea had entered his head. But you can take it from me that such a thought never occurred to him.

"Whatever his faults in the past, he is now as guileless as a child. He only wanted to get into a library. He could not bear being kept so long away from his beloved books. I promised to help him. For one moment I had the absurd idea of letting him see his children first—"

"Did Camilla come to your rooms that night?" I interrupted eagerly. "I thought I saw her on the staircase, but afterwards she disappeared. I followed her. She wasn't in the court, or the gyp's pantry or anywhere. So, unless she came in here—I must have been mistaken."

A slightly puzzled look had come over Dr. Warren's face. "No," he said slowly, "she did not come into my rooms that night. My little scheme for having her meet her father never materialized because Grayling came down to say—but you know all that.

"After we had left the Master's lodge, I drove North up to the house of a friend of mine near Oakham. He has one of the finest sixteenth century libraries in the country. Immediately after the inquest I told Horrocks the whole truth."

"About his having been here that night and about Camilla?"

Dr. Warren nodded. "Everything," he said quietly.

This then, I reflected, was the reason for Horrocks' attendance at the cricket match—the explanation of his cryptic remark to me in the court on the day of Hankin's murder.

"But Mrs. North, sir? Don't you know anything about her? Doesn't she come into this?"

The tutor shook his head. "No Fenton, but the inspector is looking for her. He's been working every night lately, poor fellow, and he's not leaving a single stone unturned."

"She couldn't be in the college—say, as a bedmaker?" I suggested nervously.

Dr. Warren smiled almost tolerantly. "Your imagination is beginning to run away with you, Fenton," he said good-humoredly. "People like Mrs. North do not become—er—bedmakers. She was a beautiful woman—a born actress and, I am afraid, a born courtesan.

"We lost track of her completely after the trial, and we are not sure now whether she is in this country, though there is reason to believe that she is. Your discovery about her third child is—or may be—a valuable contribution. I had completely forgotten the circumstances. It is all so long ago."

I paused a moment, unwilling to voice the most terrible and, at the same time, the most concrete of my suspicions. "Dr. Warren," I said hesitatingly, "if young North is here at All Saints, and if he really did this thing—well, the field is very limited—there are only five or six undergraduates who—"

"That," interposed the tutor quickly, "is also being investigated. But—" he shook his head deprecatingly, "it all seems very unlikely. Somerville's father is so well-known, a baronet of impeccable standing; Grayling's is a rector in a small Gloucestershire village; Mr. Comstock, as you know, is a manufacturer of—er—garments; and the Governor of Senegambia!

"There is hardly likely to be anything in the family history of those boys which would not bear the closest scrutiny. But, as you say, it is conceivable that young North may be an undergraduate here. I shall speak to Horrocks tomorrow. I am very glad you came to me. And now—I'm rather busy. If you will excuse me ..."

As Dr. Warren accompanied me to the door, he stopped and looked at me for a moment with a curious gleam in his eyes.

"You've gone into this matter rather deeply, haven't you, Fenton?" he said quietly. "You've thought about it pretty hard and, if I may be allowed to say so, fairly sanely. You are not your father's son for nothing. The legal mind, I suppose. Well, it helps, but remember it won't get you through your examination for the English Tripos next month. Good night."

But the night was not destined to be a good one—at least not in the conventional sense of the word. For, as I left Dr. Warren's rooms and began to climb the stairs, I almost collided with the college porter who was puffing his way downwards like a steam engine.

"Oh, Mr. Fenton," he panted, "there's a gent at the gates as wants to speak to you urgent. He sez 'e carn't come up; 'e's in a nurry, sir—a norful 'urry."

"But it's almost ten o'clock. Who on earth can it be?" I asked in surprise.

"A stranger, sir. Clean-shaven, talks with a kinda furrin accent and not so young as 'e was."

A thousand strange possibilities flashed through my mind as I followed the porter out towards the college gates. Who on earth did I know who was clean shaven and talked with a foreign accent—a middle-aged man? Could it, perhaps, be my father? William North without a beard?

Or was it—was it the unknown person who had spoken to Hankin in the court on the night he was murdered—the sinister figure who had lurked behind the lilac bush awaiting his opportunity to strike? Was some startling adventure—some strange new revelation—in store for me?

I was not kept long in doubt. Under the large lamp that lighted the main entrance to the college stood a tall, thin man, closely wrapped in a fur coat. Even when he turned and faced me, I could not immediately recall where I had seen those sallow features before. Then, suddenly, I remembered. He was the man who had given evidence at Julius Baumann's inquest—the lawyer who handled his father's estate. His name—if I recalled it rightly—was Johann Van der Walt.

CHAPTER XVII

Taximetrically Speaking

T HE lawyer advanced fussily toward me with his hand outstretched. Instead of looking at my face, however, his eyes were fixed on my wrist watch. It was two minutes before ten o'clock.

"Mr. Fenton," he cried with a pompous, rather foreign gesture, "you must forgive me for this unseasonable call—on Sunday evening too—but my business in Cambridge was urgent. And now I have to catch the ten-twenty up to town. There is a taxi waiting. Would it be too much to ask you to come with me to the station? We could, perhaps, talk in the cab undisturbed."

I noticed that, in spite of the fur coat and the season of the year, Mr. Van der Walt looked cold and pinched. He was shivering slightly.

"I should explain," he added, "that I am leaving for South Africa this week. That is why I am so anxious," he lowered his voice, "to settle my—er—business as speedily as possible. Something has come up which—"

The clock was beginning to strike the hour. It was now or never, I decided, as the porter bustled out of his lodge preparatory to closing the heavy iron gates.

"All right; I'll come. Wait a minute though. I'll get a cap and gown." I hailed an unknown youth who was hurrying to get into the college before the gates closed.

"Have a heart, Jim, and save me six and eightpence."

The young man threw off his gown with a dramatic flourish. "My name," he announced, "is Percival. I object on principle to the name of Jim. But I will overlook your inaccuracy. Here is my cap and gown. Kindly return same to Percival Fitzmonckton, C two."

"Thanks hoggish. I'm A one. Fenton's the name."

The clanging of the gate cut his rejoinder short and I joined

Mr. Van der Walt in the waiting taxi. We passed through several narrow alleys and finally emerged into the almost deserted Trinity Street. It was not until then that my companion cleared his throat, blew his nose and started to speak.

"Mr. Fenton," he said, talking hurriedly and rather jerkily in his strange, throaty accent, "you must think my behaviour is very odd, but, as I have said before, it is imperative that I catch the ten-twenty express to town. I had already waited ten minutes for you."

"That's all right, sir, but I'm sorry to have kept you waiting. I like a nocturnal taxi ride. But—"

"Yes, you may well say 'but,' Mr. Fenton. My only excuse for my—er—lapse from convention is that a rather extraordinary thing has happened—something which indirectly involves yourself. I should explain that I belong to the firm that handles the Baumann estate."

"Yes, yes. I saw you at the inquest. I remember you distinctly."

"Well, then, you will doubtless recall that Julius Baumann's farm and property reverted automatically on his death to a cousin of his father's. The settlement of that part of the estate will be very simple. I shall take it up next month after my return to Africa.

"There were, however, almost two thousand pounds to the young man's credit in his banking account not to mention some large withdrawals which he made just before his death. This money he could dispose of in any way he wished. Yesterday, to my surprise, I received through the post a document purporting to be Julius Baumann's last will and testament.

"It is written on college notepaper and dated last Monday—the day on which Julius met with his unfortunate accident. The legatee was a woman. She gave an address near Cambridge and asked if I could come to see her. She added that her present state of health did not permit her to travel. I was rather sceptical about the document, so I came in person to investigate."

Here he produced from his pocket a piece of paper. In the half light of the taxi I distinguished my own scrawled signature—H. A. Fenton, All Saints College, Cambridge, and also the name of our unfortunate gyp. Try as I would, I was unable to read what was written on the rest of the paper.

"Now, Mr. Fenton, I am naturally anxious to know if this signature is authentic. I have been given to understand that the other witness, Thomas Hankin, is recently deceased."

"That's right and my signature is perfectly okay. Baumann got Hankin and me to sign it the day he died, though whether or not he was sane and in his right mind—"

"Thank you, thank you a thousand times, Mr. Fenton. If that is so, I see no reason why the will should not be probated immediately. It is a perfectly valid legal document. The legatee can establish her identity. I have come from her house just now."

"You've seen her—the lady?" I cried excitedly. "What is her name? Where does she live?"

The taxi had now drawn up outside the dreary stretch of sheds and platform which constitutes Cambridge railway station. As the lawyer got out, I noticed a canny, almost furtive expression on his face. His eyes had narrowed into tiny slits.

"That, Mr. Fenton, I am not at liberty to tell you—at least, not until after the will has been proved. I do not wish to seem churlish, but—in the interest of my client—the less undesirable publicity—" he waved his hand airily as if to dismiss my impertinent curiosity and scatter it to the winds of heaven. "I may take it you are prepared to swear to your signature, if necessary?"

"Why yes, of course."

He handed the driver several crisp notes. "Kindly take this young gentleman wherever he wishes to go. You may keep the change. Ah! there is the express. I must run along. Good night, Mr. Fenton, and, once more, my apologies for disturbing you at this hour."

The fur coat disappeared down the platform. I turned to the youthful taxi driver, who was tucking the notes into his trouser pockets, a cheerful grin on his freckled face.

"Nice fare," I commented pleasantly.

The young man spat on his hands and rubbed them together as if to engage in a playful boxing bout.

"Well, I dunno. Been wiv 'im since the three-thirty down train. Waited for 'im an hour out t'house, too. Now, sir, where d'you want to be took?"

A brilliant, a perfectly scintillating idea flashed, crashed and hurtled through my tired brain. Mr. Van der Walt had undoubtedly come from the house of Mrs. North. He had refused to give me her name or address. But a taxi driver is a beast of burden. He is there to do what he is told; he is the nearest approach to a bond-slave that modern civilization has left us. He would take me where I wanted to go without question.

I produced a pound note from my wallet and brandished it in front of his pleasant snub nose. "I'll give you this if you take me to the same address you took that gentleman. You can get there, I suppose?"

The driver's eyes were gleaming with an unholy light. "Blimey, gov'nor, 'op in, 'op in!" he said, and before I had time to arrange my thoughts or my emotions, I was being whirled through a part of Cambridge that is not in the guide books; down gloomy streets, dark by-paths and past mean, squalid dwellings. Finally we emerged into something that, for want of a better word, one might call the country. We drew up in front of a small whitewashed cottage with a thatched roof.

"'Ere we are, sir, as Bertie said to Gertie." The driver produced a packet of Wild Woodbines from his pocket and gave me a sly wink.

"Right. I shan't be long."

I walked up a little garden path, fragrant with rambler roses and honeysuckle. There was a light burning in one of the upper windows of the cottage. I knocked loudly. No reply. I knocked again, and this time I caught the sound of shuffling footsteps coming down the stairs within. A flicker of light appeared under the door. There was a pause while a bolt was drawn back and then I heard the clanking of a heavy chain.

Another long pause followed. In the stillness of the night I could hear my heart pounding against my ribs like the beat of a bass drum. The small hairs at the back of my neck were beginning to stiffen. I had a wild desire to turn and plunge into the waiting taxi. Only the thought of Camilla made me hold my ground.

Then, suddenly, the door was thrown open and I was blinded for an instant by the light of a candle held close to my eyes. A thousand strange possibilities flashed through my brain. Then, like a farcical anticlimax in a mystery play, I heard a familiar voice say, "By hall that's 'oly, if it ain't Mr. Fenton. Well, well, Lord love a duck, and me in dishabilly and wivout me 'at on!"

I was staring into the well-known face of my bedmaker. A rosy blush had suffused her cheeks and there was an air of embarrassment about her that was almost girlish. I was completely nonplussed. The sudden apparition of Mrs. Bigger (without her hat) was too much for me. I goggled at her foolishly.

"Good—good evening, Mrs. Bigger," I stammered. "I didn't know you lived here."

"Oh, this ain't me 'ome, sir. I jes' drops in occasionally to 'elp *her*, pore soul." She gave an upward and backward jerk of her head. "She's not long for this world, Mr. Fenton, that she ain't. It's nothing as you could put your finger on exactly, but she's that wasted 'n frail. An' it's the ammonia as'll carry 'er off, sir, one of these fine days, same as it carried off me pore brother 'Arold a year ago come Michaelmas."

"Can I see her?" I asked eagerly. "I've just left the lawyer and—and—there was a message—something he forgot. It's rather important."

A look of suspicion and distrust flickered for a moment over the bedmaker's face. "I don't know as she'll see you, sir," she remarked doubtfully. "She don't see nobody as a rule ..." I had now produced two half-crowns from my pocket and slipped them deftly into Mrs. Bigger's palm. "But," she added brightening, "I can but arst 'er."

She went into the house, leaving me standing on the doorstep. I waited an interminable quarter of an hour. When the good Mrs. Bigger reappeared she wore the well-known hat with the ostrich plumes, and her dishabille was modestly hidden beneath a voluminous alpaca coat, which conformed to the University regulations in that it was of a "subfusc colour."

"Madame Nordella," she announced grandiloquently, "says she can give you ten minutes, Mr. Fenton. Step this way, please, sir."

I followed Mrs. Bigger up a narrow flight of stairs into a small upper room. A fire was burning in an old-fashioned fireplace. There were two candles on the mantelpiece and an iron bed in one corner. A woman dressed in a loose green wrapper was reclining in a large arm chair.

My first thought on entering this dimly lit room, was that its occupant could not possibly be the ill-starred Mrs. North, mother of Julius Baumann and Camilla. This woman looked young and beautiful. Her cheeks were pink and her mouth vivid red, while her hair was the colour of burnished copper.

As my eyes became accustomed to the partial obscurity, however, I saw that the colour in cheek and lips was artificial, that her overburnished hair was white at the roots and that there were deep lines around her mouth and eyes. But nothing—not even age, ill health or grease paint—could mar the splendid regularity of her features or the proud carriage of her head. The words of Dr. Warren—"a born actress"—passed through my mind.

Madame Nordella made a vague gesture in the direction of the door. "Thank you, Louisa; you may leave us now."

Mrs. Bigger shuffled out of the room. "I'll be trottin' 'ome, I reckon," she murmured. "Good night, me dear. Good night, Mr. Fenton. Now don't overtax 'er, sir. She's frail, very frail, and remember there's ammonia in these damp, misty days."

As the door closed behind her, Madame Nordella gave me a charming but not altogether convincing smile. "Well, Mr. Fenton," she said in the well-modulated voice of the stage, "won't you sit down? Mrs. Bigger tells me you are an American. Perhaps you have seen me play? I have toured America in—" she mentioned one or two musical comedies which must have been popular when I was still in the nursery. I shook my head.

She then proceeded to waste at least five of our precious ten minutes discussing stage matters in general, deploring the decay of what she called the "legit" and inveighing against the popularity of the cinema. I listened as politely as I could, but my eyes were wandering toward the mantelpiece, where I could see the photograph of a smiling girl whose features, even in that dim light, looked familiar to me. I reflected that Camilla must still have a place in Mrs. North's heart.

Apparently the former actress noticed my inattention. "But there was something special you wanted to say to me, Mr. Fenton? Some matter of business—something about the—er—will?" She started to cough and took a sip from the glass at her side. As she put down the tumbler, I plunged into the subject which was nearest my heart.

"No, no," I cried, "it wasn't about the will. I lied to Mrs. Bigger because I wanted to see you and that seemed the only way. You must believe me when I say I'm awfully glad the money is coming to you. I'll do my best to help if there is anything I can do. But I wanted to speak to you about something more important—a matter of life and death. Mrs. North ..."

At the sound of this name she drew herself up in her chair. The marvelous gray eyes stared at me coldly. "My name is Madame Nordella, if you please, Mr. Fenton," she said with dignity. "It is obvious that—" a wave of the hand completed the sentence.

"I'm sorry, I'm sorry," I stammered, "but really you can trust me. I know all about everything and I'm in love with your daughter. I've asked her to marry me. She's in great danger—terrible danger. I want you to help me. Someone is trying to kill her—just as Julius Baumann and Thomas Hankin were killed. An attempt was made on her life this very afternoon. She is threatened on all sides. She isn't safe a minute."

Throughout this speech Mrs. North had been listening to me with her eyes closed. At last she opened them and passed a weary hand across her brow.

"Mr. Fenton," she said, "there is no need for me to tell you that such subjects are very painful to me. I have had to give up a great many things in my life—and one of them is the guidance of my children. You say my daughter is in danger. I can well believe it. Cambridge is a dangerous place for our family, Mr. Fenton. I myself feel neither safe nor happy here.

"If you really love her you must get her away. I have always thought that she would be happier on the other side. With my influence over there I could easily get her into a good company. But she *would* come to Cambridge. Well, she must take her chance."

"I'll do my best to take her back to America with me," I cried eagerly, "if only she'll come. But, in the meantime, can't you give me some help in solving this terrible, ghastly riddle? Can't you tell me more about your family—something that might throw some light on this whole miserable business?" I paused and looked at her imploringly.

"Mrs. North," I cried at last, "I want you to tell me about your third child. I want you to tell me whether he is an undergraduate at Cambridge now."

Mrs. North staggered to her feet. "Mr. Fenton," she said in a strained, husky voice, "my son is dead. All my children have been taken from me except my daughter—and you know more about her, apparently, than I do. If you wish to enter into what would undoubtedly be a very unsuitable match from your point of view, you are free to do so. I have forfeited the right to interfere in the lives of my children. There's nothing else to be said. Will you be so kind as to go now."

She had fallen back into her chair and was reaching out a feeble hand toward the tumbler by her side. I handed it to her. "Thank you," she murmured. "Good night. Yes, yes, I shall be all right. Please leave me now."

I turned toward the door, too dazed to speak. As my fingers fumbled with the handle I heard a faint voice from behind me. It was a cry from the heart—this time the cry of a woman, not an actress. "If you marry her, be good to her. Remember, she hasn't ever had ... a chance."

I groped my way down the narrow stairway and out into the garden. The cool night air was like a benediction after that stuffy room. My faithful taxi driver was waiting for me. As soon as I appeared, he stubbed his cigarette on the curbstone and put it behind his ear.

"All Saints," I grunted, "and make it snappy. I must get in before midnight."

He certainly made it snappy.

After I had returned his gown to Mr. Percival Fitzmonckton, and refused his offer of a little game of Bovril, I walked wearily back to my room. I was too tired to think any more about the events of that extraordinary day.

Tired as I was, however, I could not fail to realize that, as far as useful information was concerned, I had got precisely nowhere. The case was no nearer solution than it had been the day before yesterday. Only one point stood out. Mrs. North had told me that her son was dead. Well, "dead" is a word that may be used literally or figuratively.

In any case, I had by no means discarded North Junior from my mind.

CHAPTER XVIII

Quiet Interior

W HEN I awoke next morning I was conscious of a curious sense of elation. It was Monday, the first anniversary of my meeting with Camilla. So much had happened in this one short week, and yesterday, I reflected, as I shaved myself at the spotted mirror, only yesterday I had kissed her and she hadn't seemed to mind. Of course she had promised nothing definite, but it was obvious that she didn't altogether loathe the sight of me. She didn't even seem to object much to my face.

I made grimaces at its soapy image in the looking-glass. I started to whistle and promptly cut myself on the chin. But I didn't care. Life, I observed profoundly, is like that. A whistle and then a cut—a moment of pleasure followed by a moment of pain—love and death. So it goes. So had the past week gone by.

When I entered my sitting room, shaved, washed and with a rakish piece of cotton wool saucily perched on my chin, I realized at once that all was not entirely serene in my modest establishment.

The breakfast things were not laid. I could write my name in the dust of the mantelpiece. The ashtrays still bore the mangled butts of the cigarettes which had helped to wrestle with the problem of North Junior.

Everywhere was lacking the evidence of Mrs. Bigger's loving touch. Since Hankin's death the poor bedmaker had worked valiantly at her double duty, but now her arches must have fallen once and for all. I yelled her name on every landing, but the old oaken beams of the staircase merely echoed back my words in mockery. Mrs. Bigger was nowhere to be found.

I was hungry and annoyed. Of course I could get my breakfast elsewhere, but I wanted particularly to hold a conference this morning with my ex-Egeria. There were a thousand questions that I had to ask her; but, first and foremost, I needed her assurance that my nocturnal taxi ride had not been some strange form of ambulatory nightmare.

She alone could tell me whether I had indeed talked with Madame Nordella—or Mrs. North—in that stuffy little upstairs room. And she alone could elucidate some of those extraordinary happenings of yesterday which, in the clear sunlight of a May morning, seemed utterly fantastic and remote.

And Mrs. Bigger's proudest boast had always been that despite the demises, layings-out and funerals with which her private life must have been positively cluttered, she had never—not once during her twenty years of bedmaking—deserted the inmates of "A" staircase. But now she had failed me in the hour when I needed her most.

"Frailty, thy name is Bigger," I muttered gloomily, as I finally sallied forth down the unswept and untended stairs. I perked up considerably, however, when I saw an unstamped envelope waiting for me on the bottom step. One glimpse at the writing caused my heart to give a hop, skip and a jump.

I had seen it before on the attendance list at the Blake lecture, but on that inauspicious occasion I had not had sufficient sense to attach it to its proper owner. Some instinct now told me that I was opening the nearest approach to a love-letter I had ever received in my life: and though it was not exactly couched in passionate terms, it made me very happy. It read:

Hilary Fenton, my dear, I've been thinking over what you said to me and what I said to you yesterday. I'm going to cut all lectures (even Forbes' on Blake—alas!) and do a lot more heavy thinking today. So please don't try to see me until 4:30pm at the Master's. I'm going there at four as I want half an hour alone with him first. And after that I want some time alone with you.

C. L.

P. S.—I looked up Philadelphia on the map yesterday.

As I raised my eyes from the thirteenth perusal of this precious letter, I suddenly found myself staring into the thick underbrush of Horrock's moustache. He looked more like Old Bill than ever— but now he suggested Old Bill after a week of shell-shocked nights in a far, far "better 'ole" than the Cambridge Police Station. The normal plum and apple of his complexion had changed to—shall we say pears and green gages? There was no doubt about it. The man appeared absolutely worn out.

"Hullo, Horrocks," I remarked jauntily, "you look rather green about the gills this morning."

"At any rate I can still shave without cutting myself, Mr. Fenton," he replied a trifle absently.

I removed the telltale piece of cotton wool from my chin, smiling. "Well, how are things going?" I asked with ill-concealed eagerness.

The inspector's face had now assumed the secretive, self-important expression of one who is delivering an urgent telegram, the contents of which he will not disclose to any but the right person.

"On the last lap, sir, and just coming up the straight, as you might say. At least, I think I know who was the last person to speak to Hankin in the court on Friday night."

"Is that so? Well, I can see from your face that you are not telling, but you might let me know about the teacup. Has your analyst examined it yet?"

"Yes, Mr. Fenton. We had his report this morning. There was enough prussic acid in it to poison a young elephant, let alone a pretty young lady!"

I shivered. "My God, man, aren't you going to *do* anything about it?"

A flash—the nearest approach to anger that I had ever seen— appeared for a moment in his heavy, placid face.

"*Do* anything about it, Mr. Fenton! What do you think I've been doing night and day this past week? Staying home and playing rummy with the missus? Work, Mr. Fenton, and work as I needn't have done at all if my *pals* had been a little more open with me—a little bit more confidential like you might say.

"There wasn't any reason as I can see, sir, why you shouldn't have told me about that letter you posted for Mr. Baumann on Monday night. You could have saved me a mint of trouble there, Mr. Fenton, and you didn't do no good by your secretiveness. Indeed you might have done a great deal of harm—and harm in a quarter where you'd have least liked to do mischief." Here his voice rose a trifle and the plumlike bloom began to return to his cheeks.

"I didn't press you to tell the things as concerned your own private feelings, Mr. Fenton, but I did tell you I wasn't going to stand for no hanky-panky when it was a case of murder. And now I feel I should remind you that there is such a thing as withholding material evidence and hindering an officer of the law in the performance of his duty."

This was terrible. "Horrocks," I cried, "I'm sorry, frightfully sorry you feel that way about me. But there were reasons—really there were. I gave Baumann a solemn promise that I would never tell about posting his letter and I felt in duty bound to keep my word. But now that Dr. Warren has told you the whole truth about—er—Miss Lathrop and her family, and now that she's cleared of all possible suspicion, I might just as well break down and tell you everything I know."

Here I launched forth into a full account of the various incidents which had connected me with Julius Baumann and his tragic death. I omitted nothing, overemphasized nothing and slurred nothing over. Horrock's brow cleared perceptibly as I talked, but it was not until I described the events of the previous evening that he interrupted me.

"What was the address of this cottage you went to, Mr. Fenton?" he asked surprisingly.

A sudden realization of my stupidity overwhelmed me. I hadn't the faintest idea.

"Good Lord!" I cried contritely, "I was so upset I didn't even notice. I know I came back along K. P.—but the taxi driver! He'd be sure to know. Let's go and find him."

The inspector shook his head slowly. "No time for such trifles, sir. But it's too bad, too bad—and here was I thinking that we might be able to offer you a snug little billet on the Cambridge Police Force. Well, well—" here his face broke into a broad and bushy smile, and for the first time in the history of man I caught a glimpse of his large, yellow teeth, "—it can't be helped, sir. But was it by any chance a white thatched cottage with rambler roses in the garden, an oaken front door with two knobs and upper windows a good bit smaller than the lower ones?"

"Horrocks, you are a wiz—I mean, a wizard! The night was dark and I have only a vague recollection of roses, whitewash and honeysuckle. But, now you mention them, I believe you are right about the other points, too. How on earth did you know?"

Horrocks laid a large forefinger along the side of his nose and closed one of his heavy-lidded eyes.

"One has to inquire about these little things for one's self, Mr. Fenton, since one's friends won't."

"Talking of inquiring for one's friends," said a voice behind him, "Grayling and I have just been saying that we all ought to go and inquire about the Old Pill's state of health some time today. How about it, Fenton?"

The speaker was Lloyd Comstock who was now standing alongside with Michael. The inspector nodded them good morning.

"I'm going there at four-thirty," I replied rather irritably. "Miss Lathrop is going, too."

"In that case," remarked Comstock imperturbably, "we'll have no difficulty in persuading the Honorable Somerville to come along. I heard him say this morning that she looked like the sort of cold water that runs hot if only you leave it running long enough."

A stinging retort sprang to my lips but, like jesting Pilate, my friends had not waited for an answer.

The inspector looked speculatively after their retreating figures. "I think," he said slowly, "I'll join that little party at Dr. Hyssop's this afternoon—that is, if you've no objection, sir."

"No, Horrocks, of course not, but—" I looked at him imploringly—"but don't come too early. How about five o'clock."

The detective smiled indulgently. "I'm a better pal than you are, Mr. Fenton. I know when young people want to be together. Now I must get to work. There's plenty to do!"

He moved away, but he had not gone more than three yards when he came back towards me.

"Just one little piece of advice, Mr. Fenton. A word to the wise, like you might say, sir. I wouldn't speak to the young lady about that little visit you made last night if I were you. It would only upset her and—and she's going to have plenty more trouble before we've finished.

"Besides, the party you visited was taken into Addenbrooke's Hospital this morning. Mrs. Bigger went along to keep an eye on her. I'm afraid she's pretty bad, sir, and it won't do her nor the young lady any good—well, you understand I'm sure, sir, that having been separated so long, as you might say ..."

He might have been speaking of his own mother or sister so sympathetic and kindly was his tone.

"You're dead right, Horrocks," I agreed, and he marched off through the college gateway with a brisk, military step.

He left me with a desire to go out and buy a hat so that I could take it off to the tact, industry and almost incredible acumen of Inspector Herbert Horrocks and all he stood for.

Every time I saw the inner workings of this man's mind, I was seized with a blind and almost overwhelming feeling of Anglophilia. I did not know who had murdered Baumann and Hankin—I did not know who had tried to poison Camilla—but I did know that, had I myself been the guilty party, I would rather have had Sherlock Holmes, Philo Vance and all the famous detectives of fiction on my trail, than this one stolid, solid, florid English policeman.

I repeat that I did not know who had committed these two murders, nor, when I presented myself at the Master's lodge at four-thirty that afternoon did I have any more idea than (I hope) the reader now has. My mind was still a farrago of half-formulated notions and my ideas were as foggy as yesterday's weather.

"It's all right, Mary," I said as the pretty housemaid was about to announce me. "I'll go right in. They are both expecting me."

I knocked softly at the library door and pushed it gently open. For a moment I stood on the threshold gazing at the scene in front of me.

The Master was seated in his favourite armchair by the window with Camilla on a low stool at his side. A ray of afternoon sunshine had stolen through the thick velvet curtains, catching her hair and surrounding her face with an aureole.

The old man's head was bent over hers so that his flowing white beard was also within the circle of light, which accentuated his benevolent age just as it enhanced her youth and beauty. And the old leather volumes on the shelves seemed to hold the impression, to stamp it on the memory and make it eternal.

I felt as if I were looking at the original of a peaceful interior by one of the old Dutch masters—at two figures waiting for the brush of a Rembrandt or a Hals to immortalize them and send them down through future ages as a study in contrasts.

Without intending to eavesdrop, I stood there a few minutes staring at these two. They seemed to be completely wrapped up in each other and quite unconscious of my presence. The Master was the first to break the silence and, as I listened to his words, I instinctively knew what they had been talking about and why I had been feeling so elated all that day.

"My dear, I am a grandfather—indeed, I am a great-grandfather— and if one of my grandsons or my great-grandsons were to come and tell me that he had been lucky enough to win your love, it would be one of the happiest days of my life. You need have no fears about your own family, my child. And as for the young man, I know his people, too. They are splendid folk, and he—well, he's almost like one of my own."

At this point I realized that I was listening to something which I was not altogether intended to hear. As I stepped forward, Dr. Hyssop rose from his seat and made me flatteringly welcome.

"And now," he cried, after Camilla and I had exchanged stiff, self-conscious greetings, "I am going to give you children a little treat. We might perhaps call it a celebration. No, no, it's not tea this time. It's a sip, just a sip of my very best sherry." He glanced at his clock.

"Of course, it's a trifle early for sherry, but have you ever noticed how pleasant it sometimes is to do the right thing at the wrong time? I put this particular wine in the cellar myself ten years before your father came up to Cambridge, Hilary. No one but myself is allowed to touch it, so—if you will excuse me ..."

He bustled from the room with the concentrated eagerness of a child who has gone to fetch his favourite toys.

I turned to Camilla, who was now standing by the window looking out at the roses in the fellows' gardens. For a moment we stood there together, watching a kingfisher darting to and fro along the banks of the Cam like a flash of blue-green steel in the afternoon sunlight. I moved a step nearer and the next thing I knew was that she was in my arms, that her lips were warm against mine and a few erring strands of her lovely dark hair were brushing against my cheek.

"Darling," I whispered, "I love you. I love you so. You're beautiful—like that bird—our halcyon...."

At this moment the Master reappeared bearing aloft, like a sacrificial offering, an old black bottle covered with the dust and cobwebs of past decades. He started to draw the cork with the care and precision of a surgeon performing a delicate operation.

Camilla, who had stayed by my side at the Master's entrance, now seated herself sedately on the sofa as Mary appeared with a tray and three glasses.

Dr. Hyssop made happy, satisfied little noises as he poured out the clear amber fluid into the crystal goblets. He watched their progress with zealous, almost maternal solicitude after he had handed them to the maid. She, seemingly entering into the spirit of these mystic rites, carried the tray to the sofa and bent reverentially over Camilla as she passed her a glass.

"A toast," cried our host pleasantly, when the three of us were left alone together. "Will you propose a toast, Hilary, my boy? Something worthy of the occasion?"

An idea, indeed a whole series of ideas had flashed through my head within the last few minutes. Like the ray of light which had filtered through the curtains onto Camilla's hair earlier that afternoon, a sudden inspiration had come to me, clarifying and illuminating the dark places in my mind.

I rose to my feet. "Let us drink," I said, "to a happy and speedy issue out of all our afflictions."

Then, as we raised our glasses, I added, "And I really believe that this issue will be a great deal speedier than anyone expects, because I've just had an idea, in fact, I believe I know—"

But I was interrupted at this point by the appearance of Mary Smith, who announced that Inspector Horrocks was at the front door. As we heard his heavy tread in the passage outside, the Master hurriedly refilled our glasses and whispered to me a trifle plaintively: "Do you think, Hilary, that he would appreciate—that I ought to offer him some of this sherry? There's not much of it left and ..."

"I'm perfectly certain he'd prefer stout," I replied. "Guinness is his brand, I believe."

The Master looked relieved and whispered an order to Mary. He then nodded hospitably towards the newcomer, who was immediately supplied with a large brown bottle of his favourite brew.

"Inspector Horrocks, we are just having a little celebration." Here he smiled toward Camilla and me. "I hope you will drink with us before we get down to other—perhaps less pleasant business."

"Thank you, thank you kindly, sir. My business is not what you might call pressing. It can wait, sir. Business can always wait for a glass of stout."

When all the glasses were empty, the Master resumed, "And

just before you came in, Inspector, our young American friend here was saying something rather interesting. May I suggest we give him the floor for a few moments?"

Horrocks smiled broadly, refilled his glass and performed a remarkable swallowing trick—so remarkable, indeed, that for a moment I thought the tumbler would follow the stout down his gullet or get lost in the jungle of his moustache. He then wiped his mouth, smiled again and gave me a paternal nod. "Mr. Fenton hasn't had the floor half enough for my liking, sir," he said meaningly.

I was so excited by the sudden flash of inspiration which had just come to me that I could not speak for a moment. I was conscious of three pairs of eyes staring at me expectantly, then I heard a tremulous voice, vaguely resembling my own, saying in thin, reedy tones:

"I don't know how much you know, Horrocks, but I'm pretty sure I know now who it was that killed Baumann and Hankin. And not only do I think I can prove my point, but I also believe that I'll be able to show you the actual person—for, unless I am much mistaken, the murderer is going to come into this very room ... while we are here...."

CHAPTER XIX

North Junior

But my announcement, which was intended to be quite startling and dramatic, had very little visible effect on the imperturbable Horrocks. He raised his glass calmly to his lips and took a sip of stout before speaking:

"Well, you being the amateur, as you might say, Mr. Fenton, I think an old professional like myself should stand aside for a moment and let you have the first ball. I might mention, though, sir"—here he turned apologetically to Dr. Hyssop—"that I have just sworn out a warrant. It's here in my pocket and when I leave the college tonight, someone is going to leave with me.

"There's a plainclothes constable standing at the gates now with certain orders so we needn't be afraid that anyone will give us the slip." Here he turned toward me with a nod. "And you can take your time, Mr. Fenton, take your time. To be quite frank, sir, I'm not too sure of my own ground and your story may be a help— a great help. Only, just at the moment, I'd rather you didn't name no names, sir. There are reasons why ... reasons which I'll explain later, when I have my innings."

Horrocks' calm attitude and his inability to get excited had restored, in a measure, my own composure.

"All right," I replied, "I won't mention any names until you give me the high sign, Inspector. But I would like"—I turned toward my host—"have I your permission, Master, to go over this whole business from the very beginning?"

Dr. Hyssop nodded his head and closed his eyes wearily.

"I've been a fool," I cried, "a blind, stupid fool. I've made every kind of mistake, but there is one thing I've been right about. From the very first I felt positive that the murderer was a member of this college. That must have been obvious to anyone who knew anything about college rules and regulations.

"But I couldn't see what on earth his motive was. Last night, as I told you, Inspector, I studied the history of the North family and discovered that Mrs. North had had another child who would now be about the age of the average undergraduate."

"Twenty and nine months, to be exact," murmured Horrocks.

Camilla started. "Well, I never heard of that," she exclaimed, "and I can hardly believe it. Are you quite sure, Hilary?"

"Quite sure," I replied gently. "Your—Mrs. North—had a baby a few weeks after the end of the second trial. I hate to distress you by dragging in your family this way—"

"Oh, go on, please go on!" she cried with nervous impatience. "This isn't a time to consider anyone's feelings."

"All right, then. Let's begin with William North's third child whom I've been calling North Junior in my mind ever since last evening. If no one objects, I'll go on that way. Then I needn't mention any definite names, Horrocks."

The inspector nodded. "I think you're on the right track, Mr. Fenton, but take your time, sir, take your time."

I continued: "Well, as I said before, I was quite certain that North Junior was in residence here at All Saints. He must have known about his relationship to Julius Baumann and to yourself, Camilla. Also he must have known that you both had money of your own. Money which he thought, or hoped, might eventually come to his mother and thus, at her death, to himself.

"Or perhaps he just hated you both in a blind, unreasoning way. That would be motive enough in itself when one considers the—er—unfortunate circumstances of his birth. At any rate, he planned to kill Baumann, and we all know with what fiendish cunning and precision he waited for his opportunity. He chose the night of the thunderstorm for obvious reasons.

"I believe that it was the merest coincidence that this was the day on which his father, William North, escaped from the home. But we need not go into the complications caused by this coincidence. All that concerns us is that, somehow or other, North Junior got into Baumann's room that evening—exactly how or when does not matter, but it must have been in the neighbourhood of ten o'clock.

"After this point we will simply have to draw on our imaginations. We can picture the scene when he announces his relationship; he talks with Baumann, but all the time he keeps an eye on the biscuit tin where he knows from Mrs. Bigger that the revolver is kept. He seizes his opportunity and shoots. The sound of the shot is drowned by thunder.

"Even I, and the other chaps on the staircase who were nearby at the time, could not be certain that we heard it. After his victim is dead, he plants the Brasso and the cleaning rags that he has brought with him; he arranges the revolver so that it will look like suicide or accident. Perhaps the lights are on. Perhaps he is using a flashlight, or perhaps the electricity has gone off in the middle of his gruesome operations.

"In any case, things are none too easy for North Junior. We can imagine how he looks fearfully around the room. Has he overlooked anything? Yes, he has missed one small, telltale blood stain—the one that I was foolish enough to remove later that night. He prepares to leave. The unexpected darkness, which may have complicated his carefully-planned murder, will now be an asset in that it covers his retreat.

"He goes out of the room, sporting the oak behind him so as to delay discovery of the body as long as possible. He creeps down the stairs, unnoticed—so he thinks and hopes. But Hankin must have seen or suspected something, exactly what we shall probably never know.

"Perhaps the gyp does not even realize the full importance of his suspicions until after the inquest. Perhaps he has been bribed or persuaded in some way to hold his tongue. But Hankin must go too. North Junior chooses a time when the college is very quiet. He waits until he is alone with Hankin in the court. Then he stabs...."

If I had felt any embarrassment or self-consciousness at the beginning of my monologue, I had now lost it completely. I was no longer a rather immature undergradute in the presence of the Master of his college and an experienced inspector of Police—I had projected myself completely into the personality of North Junior.

"And now he may well congratulate himself that he is safe. The coroner's verdict is on his side. Hankin is out of the way and his own identity has not yet been discovered. But there is a bitter disappointment in store for North Junior. The bulk of Baumann's property is tied up in trust funds and must go to a South African cousin.

"Only a few—a very few—hundred pounds are available—a beggarly sum in the eyes of our ambitious and unscrupulous murderer. He must look elsewhere for money. And so he turns his attention toward his sister. She has a little income of her own—an income which, he hopes, may, by some devious bypaths, eventually come to him or to his family.

"But how can he see his sister without arousing her suspicions? His chance comes sooner, perhaps, than he anticipates. He is to be present at a tea party here in this room. He conceives the idea of sending a forged invitation to Camilla for the same party. Somehow or other he gets into the Master's office, steals an invitation card and sends it to Newnham. He has also managed to extract some prussic acid from the science laboratory."

I broke off in my story, for, at this moment, the maid came into the room with a tray and began to collect up the glasses.

There was a minute of uneasy silence. The only sounds in the Master's library were the ticking of the clock, the tinkle of glasses on the tray and the frantic buzzing of a bluebottle on the window pane.

It was Camilla who finally broke the spell. Throughout my recital she had been staring unseeingly at the bluebottle's frantic efforts to escape into the sunshine and apparently she had been listening to me with such absorption that she was not aware of the maid's presence in the room.

"Oh, go on, Hilary," she cried. "What does it matter *how* he did it? Why don't you tell us *who* it was? I want to know ... a member of my own family ... you said ... you promised he would come into the room...."

Her voice broke off with a snap. I turned questioningly toward the inspector. Very slowly and deliberately he raised a finger to the side of his nose and nodded his head in a gesture of assent. Then he rose ponderously to his feet and took up his position with his back to the door. I noticed that one large hand had found its way into his coat pocket in which there was a suspicious-looking bulge.

"Camilla," I said slowly, with my eyes fixed on the inspector, "I did promise you that North Junior would come into this room while we were here. Well, my promise has been kept. The murderer of Julius Baumann and Thomas Hankin is ... in ... the ... room ... at this ... very ... moment."

There was a resounding crash of breaking glass. Mary Smith had dropped the tray and was standing behind the sofa with her hands hanging helplessly by her sides. Instead of looking down at the tray, however, she was staring at me with a strange expression of horror and bewilderment.

I jumped up from my seat and, pulling a large handkerchief from my pocket, threw it over the housemaid's glorious red hair. Then, taking her gently by the shoulders, I pushed her nearer to the couch until her head was within a few inches of Camilla's.

"Look, Master," I cried, as my grip on the girl's shoulders tightened. "Don't you see it now—the same profile? Hide the red hair and they might almost be twins. Now is there any doubt as to who it was I saw on 'A' staircase last Monday night? Now do you see why Hankin was unwilling to come forward and voice his suspicions?

"Now do you see how easy it was for the murderer to get hold of the cleaning materials—the invitation card—the prussic acid from the laboratory to which Hankin had the key? Who had a better opportunity to poison Camilla's tea yesterday afternoon? Who but North Junior—the third child of William North? Only *instead of being a boy she happened to be a girl.*"

I released my hold on Mary Smith's shoulders. She stood perfectly still, staring straight in front of her as if in a daze. At length she spoke, and I immediately noticed that her accent, which was usually that of an uneducated working girl, was now perfect in pitch and intonation.

"You ... can't ... prove ... a ... thing," she cried; and then, more shrilly, "I don't know what you mean. Oh, how dare you put your hands on me!"

At this moment the door behind Horrocks was pushed open and a powerful, thickset man entered the room. He handed the inspector a bottle which I immediately recognized from its quaint shape as being one that had originally held that fatal perfume, Flowers of the Veld.

"We found this in her room, sir," he said, smiling grimly. "You've only got to smell it to tell that it ain't the sweet perfume it's supposed to be."

"All right, Brown." Horrocks jerked his head in the direction of Mary Smith. "You can stand by."

He then unstoppered the bottle, sniffed at it gingerly and handed it to me. For the second time in that room the odour of peaches and bitter almonds assailed my nostrils.

The inspector was now addressing the maid, whose eyes were darting envenomed glances in all directions. Her cheeks were pale as death, but in spite of the fact that she had not yet removed my ridiculous handkerchief from her head, she looked a handsome and imposing figure for tragedy.

"You say we can't prove a thing, Miss," he said softly. "Well, it strikes me you are going to have a job proving why you kept prussic acid in your bedroom." He turned deferentially toward the Master. "We took the liberty, sir, of having this young woman's belongings searched while she was down here waiting on you. That was why I didn't want any names mentioned before I was ready."

Here he cleared his throat and, when next he spoke, his voice had changed from that of a kindly middle-aged man to the stern, official tones of a police inspector. He drew a document from his pocket.

"Mary North, alias Mary Nordella, alias Mary Smith, I arrest you in the King's name for the murder of Julius Baumann on Monday last, May 9th. And it is my duty to warn you that anything you say may be used in evidence." There was a slight pause, then, "Take her out, Brown, and wait in the car. Don't make any more fuss than you can help. I'll join you in a few minutes."

"I'll go quietly," murmured the girl. "Just give me one moment." She moved a step toward me and looked up into my face with an expression that was at once arch and sinister. The phrase "a born courtesan" which Dr. Warren had applied to her mother flashed immediately through my mind.

"Oh, you needn't be afraid," she exclaimed scornfully, as Brown moved up behind her and touched her elbow. "I wouldn't hurt your poor little American. He's done his best with his theories and his North Juniors and his fine long speeches, which I'm sure—" she looked impudently around her—"we've all listened to with great interest.

"You sounded fine from the other side of the door, Mr. Fenton, especially when it came to a question of motive!" Here she gave a hoarse, unpleasant laugh, and as she did so, I felt I could never apologize sufficiently to Camilla for having said that, even superficially, they resembled each other.

"But there are other things besides money, Hilary Fenton— things which perhaps you might understand better if you'd spent your young life traipsing around after a second-rate actress in cheap American and Canadian boarding houses—having fat, vulgar men smirk at you and pinch you and breathe garlic all over you— and often without enough to eat while your brother and sister, who are no better than you, are living a comfortable existence among ladies and gentlemen, with rich friends, good food and clothes, getting the benefit of education—getting the money that they had no more right to than I had. Was it my fault that my father—"

But here Inspector Horrocks stopped her. "Remember, I warned you, Miss," he said curtly. "Now, if you are ready ..."

"All right, all right, but—please, don't touch me." Then with one last vindictive look of hatred toward Camilla and myself, she walked out of the room closely followed by the hard-faced Brown.

After they had left, the Master stirred uneasily in his chair.

"I'd never have noticed it—never!" he remarked. "The resemblance, I mean—but when you mentioned it, Hilary, then, of course I saw at once that there *is* some similarity in the lines of the face."

"Well, sir," I rejoined, a trifle foolishly, "I'll admit I never would have noticed it either if it hadn't just happened that the first view I ever got of Miss Lathrop was her profile. It—er—made a great impression on me.

"When I saw that girl bending over the sofa just now with a glass of sherry, the likeness struck me at once in spite of the different colouring and expression. Then I thought of the person whom I had seen on the stairs last Monday and I suddenly realized that expression and colouring are two things that don't show in the dark."

There was a muffled sound from the sofa. As I turned toward Camilla, I noticed that the tears were streaming down her cheeks. "Poor thing!" I heard her murmur.

The Master had heard her, too, and hurried across the room to her side. I saw that he had taken her hand in his and was whispering in her ear. Obviously it was best to leave these two alone for a while. I joined Horrocks at the far end of the room.

"Well, Mr. Fenton," he remarked with a quiet chuckle, "you took the high road and I took what you might call the low road and we both got to Scotland about the same time, eh?"

"Scotland Yard is where you ought to get to, Horrocks," I cried admiringly. "I can't think how you did it—especially with everyone working against you the way they did."

"But I don't want you to go off with the idea that I didn't make mistakes too, sir. I wasted two whole days on your friend, Mr. Lloyd Comstock—on account of his first name being the same as the girl who figured in the North case. I even went all the way to Leicester where his father makes those garments that you see advertised so much, and all I got out of it was—" he lowered his voice discreetly—"three pairs of them Comfy-Knicks, sir, and they're all too small for my missus!"

I laughed immoderately.

"Then, having started on names, sir, it struck me that the name Smith was a bit suspicious. In my business, Mr. Fenton, we always mistrust anyone called Smith or Jones, unless, of course, the party can't help it. And in this case it seemed odd that the girl's name should be Smith and the mother's Nordella.

"Then I didn't altogether like that cock and bull story of hers about someone speaking to Hankin in the court and her not even listening to a word they said! If she didn't listen, then she's the first housemaid in my experience as didn't—especially when she had the keyhole close to her ear, like you might say, Mr. Fenton.

"This morning I got the girl's record from the Canadian authorities. She's been on the stage since she was a kid, except when she was doing a two years' term in the penitentiary."

"Gosh!" I cried, "and I bet she was a corking good actress, too. With her nerve and brain she might have got anywhere. No wonder I thought North Junior was a man! Not that that was the only mistake I made. Take the perfume, for example.

"Why the girl in the shop told me that it was an older man who had bought *Flowers of the Veld* there—a man with a different kind of accent. What an ass I was to jump to the conclusion that it must have been Baumann! Of course it was Hankin who was buying his own native scent for that precious girl of his! The bottle you found in her room proves it. And what a lovely use she put it to!

"Then I might have realized when I saw Mrs. Bigger out at the cottage last night that there would be some hook-up there. Mary Smith was a great pal of hers. She was always singing her praises and I'm perfectly certain that neither the bedmaker nor her own mother suspected her true nature.

"Lord, and how Mrs. North and I talked at cross purposes last night! I suppose she thought it was Mary I was keen on. And then that photograph on the mantelpiece! What a fool I was! And yet the solution was lying right under my nose the whole time!"

"Come, come, Mr. Fenton, you mustn't be too modest, you know. You've been a great help, sir—a great help. If you hadn't told me all that in the court this morning, I don't believe I'd have had enough grounds to take out a warrant. It was your seeing her on the stairs that settled it in my mind once and for all."

"And there's one point that still stumps me," I interrupted. "Where on earth did she get to that night after she passed me? I chased down after her hell for leather but she'd vanished into thin air. She wasn't in the court or the gyp's pantry or—anywhere. And what's more, she didn't leave the college until Mrs. Fancher and Mrs. Bigger did about ten minutes later on."

"Well, I dare say there's a good deal more to be cleared up before we can get a conviction, Mr. Fenton. I'll be coming round to see you tomorrow, sir, and then I'll tell you where we stand. Now I must be getting along. Good day, everyone."

With a solemn nod in the direction of the Master and Camilla, the inspector let himself out by the door. He returned almost immediately.

"There are three young gentlemen asking for you at the front door, Dr. Hyssop," he said diffidently. "Mr. Somerville, Mr. Grayling and Mr. Comstock. Shall I let them in, sir?".

The Master looked piteously toward me. "Please, Hilary, my boy, give them my compliments and tell then that I am a trifle indisposed. I think I'd like to be alone to read *Rabbi Ben Ezra* through before dinner. This sad business has rather made me feel the liabilities of my age, and perhaps Browning will help me to realize some of its compensations. Thank you—it's that red book on the third shelf. Good-bye, my children. Good-bye and God bless you both."

When Camilla and I stepped out into the late afternoon sunshine, we found Comstock, Grayling and Somerville on the front doorstep in a state of prodigious excitement. They had seen

Mary Smith go off with the plain-clothes man and they naturally pressed us with questions.

As I looked at their eager ingenuous countenances, I found it almost impossible to believe that I had ever entertained such terrible suspicions of these clear-eyed English youths. They listened with absorbed interest as I told them as much of the story as I could without implicating Camilla or disclosing her family history.

When I came to the end of my recital I noticed that Somerville's usual expression of jaunty self-assurance had changed to one of incredulous horror and bewilderment. He was biting his fingernails nervously. As the others broke forth into a stream of chatter and comment, he beckoned me aside with an urgent gesture.

"So you thought it was a ghost you saw on 'A' staircase last Monday night?" he whispered.

I nodded cautiously.

"Oh, my Lord," he groaned, "and I could have explained it so easily if I'd known—that is, if I'd known there was any suspicion of foul play about Baumann's death. I never said anything because, well, because"—he was hanging his head and looked thoroughly ashamed of himself—"I didn't see any possible connection—"

"What on earth are you driving at, Stuart?" I asked impatiently.

He paused a moment before replying and then drew me a few paces further away.

"Well, on Monday night," he said in a low, mysterious voice, "after the lights went out, I ran downstairs to my room to get a flashlight. I was just coming up again to finish my ghost story—and the whisky—when I suddenly ran bang smack into a sweet-smelling female right outside my own door.

"Having almost knocked her down, I naturally had to put my arms round her to—well—to steady her. I could feel at once that she was young and tender. And she didn't seem to object particularly. Then I heard you coming down the stairs, so I quickly pulled her into my room. I kissed her once or twice and then—all of a sudden—the lights went on again.

"I had an awful shock when I saw who it was. She was upset, too. She declared she thought I was Hank; she begged me not to tell; she said she'd lose her position and, well—I never saw any reason why I should tell, anyhow ... at least, not until now. It would have been rather caddish."

"Gosh, man, you were lucky you didn't get a knife in your ribs,"

I cried. "She must have had one with her. She probably took the Kaffir dagger from Baumann's room that night and afterwards used it to kill Hank. You'd better be careful how you kiss strange females in the dark in the future, Stuart."

He ran a hand through his hair, half smiling, half abashed.

"I'm not altogether sure it wouldn't have been worth it," he muttered. "What a perfectly ripping death! In the middle of a long ling-g-gering kiss. Um-*ah!*"

"Stuart, you really are rather repulsive," I said smiling, "but you have at least cleared up what, for me, was the most baffling part of the whole business. The way she seemed to disappear that night was positively spooky. And coming on top of that creepy yarn about your Marlborough friend! Incidentally, now that you've solved my little mystery, I wish you would tell me the end of that one. It was a darn good story."

Somerville grinned. "I'm afraid the actual dénouement is a bit of a flop. The wretched lad ought to have died on his eighteenth birthday by rights—but he didn't do anything so sweet and simple. What he actually did was to lose all his hair and he woke up next morning as bald as the jolly old curate's egg.

"And incidentally, he's up at Oxford now, poor devil—going to be a parson, too! He might just as well have pipped it at the proper time and given the story a decent ending. However, as far as I know, there's been no return of that particular nightmare."

I looked at my watch.

"Well, and let's hope our little nightmare is over, too. And now I've got to run along. I want to—er—see a jeweller about a ring."

"Before the hot water runs cold, eh?" There was a momentary return to the mocking, moviesque accent. "Well, I reckon that's a cute chick you picked."

"Quit calling my babe a chick," I parried in what at Cambridge still passed for jive talk.

"Hit the road, Frog."

And with this utterly British slang malapropism we turned to rejoin the others.

THE END

Lightning Source UK Ltd.
Milton Keynes UK
UKOW06f1213090216

268017UK00001B/94/P